"They took her. They have my sister..."

"Do you know who they were?" Becker cupped Olivia's cheek in one hand, brushing away the tears. "Can you describe them?"

Olivia shook her head. "I think they wore ski masks, but they were covered in dust. When I tried to stop one of them, he slammed me against the wall. I must have blacked out for a second or two."

Becker frowned down at her. He brushed his thumb gently across the bruise forming on her right temple. "If you blacked out—"

Olivia grabbed his hand and captured his gaze with her own green one. "They took my sister. I'm not going anywhere but to find her. It might already be too late. The people who are after her are only after one thing."

"And what's that?" Becker asked.

"She witnessed a murder." Olivia stared up at him, her voice shaking as she added, "A dead witness can't testify..."

MISSING WITNESS AT WHISKEY GULCH

New York Times Bestselling Author
ELLE JAMES

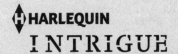

For my mother, who loved to read and showed what fun it was to get lost in a story. Wish I could pick up the phone and call you. I love and miss you, Mom.

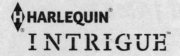

HARLEQUIN®
INTRIGUE™

ISBN-13: 978-1-335-58288-1

Missing Witness at Whiskey Gulch

Copyright © 2022 by Mary Jernigan

Recycling programs for this product may not exist in your area.

For questions and comments about the quality of this book, please contact us at CustomerService@Harlequin.com.

Harlequin Enterprises ULC
22 Adelaide St. West, 41st Floor
Toronto, Ontario M5H 4E3, Canada
www.Harlequin.com

Printed in U.S.A.

Elle James, a *New York Times* bestselling author, started writing when her sister challenged her to write a romance novel. She has managed a full-time job and raised three wonderful children, and she and her husband even tried ranching exotic birds (ostriches, emus and rheas). Ask her, and she'll tell you what it's like to go toe-to-toe with an angry 350-pound bird! Elle loves to hear from fans at ellejames@earthlink.net or ellejames.com.

Visit the Author Profile page at Harlequin.com.

CAST OF CHARACTERS

Becker Jackson—Former Delta Force soldier who retired from active duty after a helicopter crash left him with lasting mental scars and PTSD. Now working for Outriders.

Olivia Swann—Artist who crafts one of a kind pottery sought after nationwide.

Jasmine Swann—Curator at a swanky Dallas art gallery and Olivia's younger sister.

Trace Travis—Former Delta Force who shares his inheritance with his father's bastard son and builds a security agency employing former military.

Irish Monahan—Former Delta Force soldier who left active duty to make a life out of the line of fire. Working for Trace Travis as a member of the Outriders.

Matt Hennessey—Prior service, marine and town bad boy, now half owner of the Whiskey Gulch Ranch and the Outriders Agency.

Vincenzo Salvatore—Wealthy Italian American with mafia connections.

Nico Salvatore—Vincenzo's son, accused of murdering Eduardo Romano.

Giovanni Romano—Wealthy Italian American with mafia connections and a rivalry relationship with the Salvatores.

Lana Etheridge—Nico Salvatore's lover.

Briana Salvatore—Nico Salvatore's estranged wife.

Chapter One

Olivia Swann wrapped her fingers around the spinning clay, molding and shaping it into the custom vase she'd promised a wealthy client in Peoria, Pennsylvania.

In the back of her little shop, in Whiskey Gulch, Texas, she smiled at the thought of her work finding homes in places all over the US and other countries around the world.

It helped that she was a gifted artist, though she seldom thought of herself as such. Sure, she made beautiful pottery. What helped even more was having a sister who worked in a high-end art gallery in Dallas that displayed unique works of art that lured art enthusiasts from around the world.

It'd been a miracle that her sister, Jasmine, had gotten Olivia's work included.

Now she had more work than she knew what to do with—so much that in order to deliver any on time, she had to be selective in what projects she commissioned. Because of the popularity of her decorative vases, bowls and platters, she had been able to remodel her shop and her parents' home, bringing it up to the current century in style and habitability.

Jasmine loved the updates. Their mother would have loved it. Her father…not so much. He'd resisted change, insisting on keeping outdated furniture and his favorite easy chair, much to their mother's frustration. She couldn't argue too much. They'd loved each other until parted by death…a day that had come all too soon.

Olivia dipped her hands in the murky water beside her. She placed them on the damp clay and continued shaping, pulling and forming the large vase on the potter's wheel. The hum of the motor and her focus on the clay calmed her in a way nothing else could match. She was in her element, living the life she was meant to live, free of worry and the complications of relationships.

Since a failed engagement to her high school sweetheart, she'd sworn off men. Her parents' deaths had pushed dating and love to the bottom of her priority list. Olivia honestly thought she couldn't possibly find a love like her parents had enjoyed.

They'd been perfectly matched: both artistic, both free-spirited—and so into each other, no one else existed.

Not Mike. He'd said he loved her and wanted to marry her, but he hadn't stopped looking around. Especially when on one of the many conferences he attended in Vegas as part of his job.

Olivia had happened to be in his apartment when he was in the shower, getting ready for their date, and a text came through from a woman by the name of Kiki Cox.

Curious about the name, she'd looked her up online, only to find she was a hooker in Vegas.

When she'd confronted him—purely out of curiosity, never suspecting he'd strayed—she'd been stunned when he admitted to having a pre-wedding fling with the woman. Mike had assured her he was just sowing wild oats, and it wouldn't happen again after they were married.

Olivia had calmly removed the engagement ring, handed it to him and left. She hadn't talked to him since. That had been three years ago.

Other than the biological clock ticking in her ear, reminding her she had wasted some of the best years of her reproductive life, she had no regrets.

If she ever married, it would be to someone who didn't feel the need to look elsewhere for love or sex.

The bell over the shop door rang as a man entered and stood still, waiting for his vision to adjust from the harsh Texas sunlight to the cooler, dimmer interior.

Olivia glanced up from her project, her breath catching in her throat at the sight of a tall, muscular man with broad shoulders, striking ice-blue eyes, a military haircut and a scruffy five-o'clock shadow. Wow.

The vase on the wheel wobbled against her fingertips, reminding her to focus on the task. She glanced down, recovered the project—just barely—and asked, "Can I help you?"

"I'm looking for a present for my mother."

Not only was he an outstanding physical form but he also loved his mother. How much more perfect could the man be? Sigh… He was still a man. Men had faults, as she well knew.

"I'm in the middle of a project. Have a look around. If you see something you think she might like, I should be at a stopping point in a few minutes."

She risked another glance, her pulse quickening.

The man's eyes narrowed. "I hear a voice, but I don't see who it belongs to."

Olivia chuckled, returning her attention to the vase. "I'm at the back of the shop, working."

She could hear footsteps nearing her work area. The man came to a halt in front of her. "Ah, there you are."

When she glanced up, her breath caught… and she couldn't help staring.

He smiled, a twinkle in his blue eyes. "Hey."

Her heart thumped against her ribs. "Hey." Her hands shifted, and the vase she'd been working on wobbled once more and flopped over as it whirled on the wheel.

"Damn!" Olivia switched off the motor and stood up, looking down at the mess.

"Wow," he said in his deep voice. "I'm sorry. I should have done like you asked and waited until you were finished."

She sighed. "It's okay. I'll just start over." *When I'm not distracted by a drop-dead gorgeous guy taking up all the air in the shop.* She didn't say it out loud, but she was sure thinking it. "A gift for your mother, you said?"

He nodded. "Yes, ma'am. She appreciates handmade items, being that she makes things as well."

Olivia's heart warmed. "What kinds of things does she make?"

"Nothing as difficult as these," he said, sweeping his hand out to encompass the contents of her shop. "She knits blankets for foster children and beanies for newborns. But she's been collecting unique pottery, displaying it around her house in San Antonio. I think the items in your shop would be right up her alley."

"Let me wash my hands, and I'll help you." Olivia hurried to the sink at the back of the shop and washed away the residual mud from her elbows to her fingertips. Once she'd dried her hands, she checked her reflection in the mirror, her eyes widening. She had a spot of clay on her nose, which she quickly wiped away before turning back to smile at the man, who was waiting patiently.

His lip quirked upward on one side. "You missed a spot." He reached out and brushed his thumb over a smudge on her chin.

Heat rose up her neck. She raised her hand to where his was, bumping into his fingers. "Here?"

He shook his head. "No." Wrapping his fingers around hers, he guided her hand.

Warmth spread throughout her body at his touch. With her cheeks on fire, she scrubbed at her chin and dragged her gaze from his striking blue eyes. "Did you see something you liked?" she asked, anxious to draw attention away from her dirty face to the contents of her shop.

"Actually, yes."

His deep voice sent shivers up and down Olivia's spine. She shot a glance back at him to discover he was looking at her, not her pottery.

Her heart thumped hard in her chest. Her reaction to this man was getting more and more ridiculous by the minute. If he didn't leave soon, she'd be begging to have his baby.

What was wrong with her? Olivia shook her head. He was just a man—and therefore, like most men she'd run across, probably not trustworthy, most likely overbearing and possibly narcissistic. She didn't need to fall all over herself because one man was extremely ruggedly attractive and had a voice that could melt chocolate on a frosty day.

No, Olivia had renounced men after Mike. She considered herself better off without the complications of relationships. Trust wasn't easy for her.

He paused in front of one of her slender three-foot-tall vases in stunning shades of cobalt blue and black. The piece was displayed in a glass cabinet to keep people from handling it. She'd sold one like it to a wealthy client in Dallas during an art show Jasmine had curated. The vase she'd been shaping on the wheel would be similar.

"This one is beautiful," he said in that tone that made Olivia's knees weaken. He glanced her way. "You made this? You're Olivia?" Before she could answer, he shook his head. "Of course you're Olivia. You were making another creation when I interrupted. I might as well be a bull in a china shop." He clasped his hands behind his back. "I'll leave all the touching to you."

His words inspired a shiver of awareness to ripple across her skin. An image of her hands running across his broad chest made heat build at her core.

Maybe swearing off men was a bit drastic. She didn't have to commit to any one man.

"What kind of pottery does your mother like?"

He shrugged those broad shoulders. "She has a couple of large bowls. One she uses for fruit. The other is front and center on her coffee table. She has a colorful array of platters hung on her wall. What she doesn't have is a vase like this." He nodded toward the cobalt blue vase in the glass cabinet. "This vase would make her happy."

Her mouth twisted into a wry grin. "Perhaps we should start with how much you want to spend on this gift?"

His brow wrinkled. "That much, huh?"

She nodded. "The techniques and materials used to create that particular color combination are expensive and time-intensive."

"I can only imagine," he said. "It's an impressive piece. My mother visited an art gallery in Dallas. When I told her I was coming to work in Whiskey Gulch, she insisted I look for the artist she discovered at that gallery." He grinned. "Olivia Swann was the name she gave me." The man held out his hand. "My mother will be thrilled I actually met you. I'm Becker Jackson. My mother is Linda Jackson."

Olivia took his hand. "Nice to meet you, Mr. Jackson."

"Becker." He smiled. "Mr. Jackson was my father." He held her hand a little longer than necessary, his eyes narrowing as he stared down into her face. "I didn't expect Mom's artist to have such pretty green eyes."

Her cheeks burned. She wanted to tell him that he had the prettiest blue eyes, but thankfully, her tongue was too tied to make coherent conversation.

"Look…" he said, still holding her hand, "I just got to town. I don't know anyone. You wouldn't happen to want to have dinner with me, would you?"

Her brows shot up.

He chuckled. "You can tell me to get lost if I'm asking too soon, but I like your grip and your eyes. And I don't like to eat by myself." He paused. "That is, if you're alone… I mean, not married or you don't have a significant other." He scrubbed his spare hand through his hair. "Wow, talk about a lousy first impression." He pressed a kiss to her knuckles and let go. "Let me start over."

Becker performed an about-face and marched out of the shop, the bell reverberating throughout the space.

Olivia shook her head, her hand still tingling where he'd touched her. "What the hell just happened?"

Before she could form another thought, Becker entered her shop again.

"Hi," he said. "I'm looking for Olivia Swann." He winked.

Olivia frowned. "I'm Olivia. But then, you already know that."

"Humor me. I feel like a putz." He crossed the room and held out his hand. "I'm on a mission to find a gift for my mother. She won't settle for anything less than an Olivia Swann creation."

She tentatively took his hand. "I'm not sure I can help you." Her lips twitched at the corners.

"If you're Olivia, I know you can." He nodded toward the black-and-blue vase. "That vase will do. Is it for sale?"

Olivia nodded.

He let go of her hand and pulled his wallet from his back pocket. "How much do I owe you?"

"Three thousand, five hundred dollars."

Becker dropped his wallet on the ground.

Olivia laughed. "I have other vases not quite as expensive."

He scooped his wallet off the floor. "I need to have a talk with my mother about her spending all of my inheritance." Becker winked. "Seriously, I still want it. It'll have to be her birthday and Christmas present for the next five years."

Olivia shook her head. "Don't feel obligated to purchase the vase. I'd feel awful if I broke your bank."

He pulled out a credit card. "Take plastic?"

"I do."

"Can you ship it?"

She took the card from him, nodding. "Yes, I can."

"Insured?"

"Absolutely." Her frown deepened. "Are you sure?"

"Absolutely." He pulled out a card and scribbled a name and address on the back. "Here. You can have my very first business card, with my mother's address."

She stared down at the front of the card. "Outrider Security?" Olivia glanced up. "Isn't that Trace Travis's security company?"

Becker nodded. "It is. Tomorrow is my first day with them. He sent my business cards ahead to lure me in."

"Is that all it took? A few business cards with your name on them?" she asked.

He spread his arms wide. "I'm here, aren't I? You're my first stop before I head out to the Whiskey Gulch Ranch to meet up with my new boss."

"Won't he want to take you to dinner?" she asked.

"I secured a room in town for the night. I won't meet up with him until tomorrow morning." He lifted his chin. "Don't feel obligated to go out with me just because I bought a vase. I'll be fine on my own." He looked out her front window. "Though I *would* like a recommendation for a place to grab a bite."

"The diner is always good," Olivia said. "And if you still want me to join you, I'd like that. My refrigerator is all out of leftovers."

"In that case, I'm delighted to be your second choice over leftovers." He grinned. "Want me to pick you up at six? Or, if it makes you feel better, we could meet at the diner at six."

"I'll meet you at the diner at six. I need to clean up before I eat." She stepped behind the counter, ran his card through her credit card processor and handed it back to him with the receipt for him to sign. "And I'll ship your mother's vase to her on my way home."

Becker grinned once more. "Thank you. Then

I'll see you at six. And if you don't show up, I'll know I made a helluva first impression on you, and you had the good sense to stay home and eat popcorn."

She laughed. "Are you always this…?"

"Charming? Adorable? Sexy?"

"Maddening? Exasperating? Incorrigible?"

Becker winced. "Ouch. And I was leaning toward *sexy*."

Olivia waved toward the door. "Go on. I still have to close up shop, shower and change if I want to get to the diner by six."

His face brightened, a twinkle shining in his blue eyes. "So you're not discouraged."

She fought hard to keep from smiling and failed miserably. "If I say I'll be there… I'll be there."

He took her hand again, raised it to his lips and brushed the backs of her knuckles once more. "I'll be counting the minutes. Until then…" He left the shop, the bell ringing over the door.

As soon as the man was gone, Olivia let go of the breath she'd been holding and giggled like a schoolgirl.

Had she just said yes to having dinner with him?

Yes. She had.

After years of refusing to have anything to

do with men, a stranger had walked through her shop door, and she'd reneged.

But now that she'd said she'd be there, she would make good on that promise.

A glance at the clock made her yelp. Five after five? If she was going to make it to the diner by six, she had to get moving.

Olivia locked the front door, flipped the Open sign over to Closed and hurried to package the beautiful vase for Becker's mother. She had until five thirty to get it to the FedEx drop point.

Using copious amounts of Bubble Wrap and foam packaging, she wrapped the beautiful vase and placed it in a box.

After moving the clay on her wheel into a bucket to keep it moist, she washed her hands and carried the box out to her slate gray Jeep Wrangler.

The drive across town didn't take long. Whiskey Gulch wasn't that big. Olivia arrived at the shipping store in time to send the box out to the address Becker had given her. After insuring the vase and paying to ship the gift, she hurried back to her Jeep and drove to the opposite end of town and parked in the driveway of the house she'd inherited from her parents.

Once inside, she shed her clothes as she ran through the house to the en suite in the master bedroom. She was in and out of the shower in under ten minutes, with fifteen minutes to spare. She'd have just enough time to dress, dry her hair and dab on a bit of makeup before she had to race to the diner to be there by six.

Why had she agreed to have dinner with Becker at six?

Because the twinkle in his blue eyes had utterly captivated her, and she couldn't wait to see him again.

Was she insane? Hadn't she learned men couldn't be trusted?

"It's only dinner," she said as she stepped out of the shower. She dried off and wrapped the towel around her body.

A sudden creaking sound came from another part of the house.

Olivia froze, straining to hear it again. The house had been built in the early 1940s. No manner of updates would change the fact that it still made noises when the wind blew and when it didn't.

She heard a soft thump that sounded like someone running into a wall.

She raced across the bedroom to the nightstand and grabbed the baseball bat she kept by the bed. Her heart racing, she crept over to her open bedroom door and leaned out.

Now wasn't the time to remember she'd disconnected her landline phone. Nor was it a good time to remember her cell phone was in the kitchen on the counter, where she'd dropped her purse and keys.

Olivia peered down the hall.

Nothing seemed out of the ordinary.

Click.

Did someone just close my back door?

Olivia had two choices: She could go into the kitchen, possibly confront an intruder, and risk being attacked, subdued, raped and killed. Or she could branch off the hallway before reaching the kitchen, run out the front door into the yard and yell for help. She'd have to run a block; her closest neighbor was deaf.

With the bat gripped tightly in her hands, Olivia inched out into the hallway, afraid to breathe, lest she miss hearing something.

Chapter Two

Olivia's pulse pounded so hard through her veins, it thundered in her ears. She tensed her muscles, ready to make a dash for the front door and out into the open.

Before she took the first step, a strangled sob sounded from the kitchen.

"Olivia?" a faint, feminine and familiar voice called out.

She knew that voice. It was the voice she'd grown up with—her sister's.

Still carrying the bat, Olivia ran for the kitchen. "Jasmine?" As she entered the room, a hand reached out, snagged her arm and dragged her to the floor.

Her first instinct was to shake free of the grip, but fingers dug into her skin and refused to release her.

Olivia dropped to her knees beside her sister and stared into her tear-streaked face.

"Jasmine, sweetie." She cupped her sister's cheek, which was smeared with dirt and scratches. "What happened?" She hadn't heard from her in three weeks. Guilt tugged at her gut. She'd been so busy with her work, she hadn't picked up her cell phone to call Jasmine.

"I'm in trouble," she whispered.

"Do we need to get you to a doctor?" Olivia tried to stand.

Jasmine stopped her. "No. I can't," she said, choking on her words. Tears welled in her eyes. "I'm scared."

Olivia sat back on the floor with her younger sister and pulled her into her arms. "Why? What's wrong?"

"I witnessed a m-murder." Jasmine used her balled fist to cover her mouth. "I witnessed a murder, Olivia."

Olivia's stomach roiled at the horror reflected in her sister's face. "Oh, baby."

"I had returned to the gallery because I'd left my phone on my desk there. The back door was open. I knew I'd locked it and set the alarm, but it was open. The alarms were disengaged. When I went inside, I saw… I saw them. They were arguing. I recognized Nico Salvatore. He'd been in the gallery earlier that day. I didn't know the other guy. I've since learned it was Eduardo Romano. Romano had something in his hand that looked like a painting. It was wrapped in brown paper, but it was the shape of a picture frame. I wanted to tell him to put it back, but I couldn't. They didn't see me. If they had…"

"You were right not to say anything," Olivia said, thankful her sister had kept quiet.

"Maybe if I had spoken up, Eduardo would still be alive."

"Or both of you would be dead."

Her sister drew in a shaky breath. "I was scared. They were both bigger than me. I didn't have any way to protect myself, so I hid behind a cabinet and waited for them to leave. I was going to call the police then."

"You did the right thing."

Her blue eyes widened, and her bottom lip trembled. "But I saw everything."

"Oh, Jaz." Olivia held her sister's hands.

"The man with the painting turned to leave. Nico grabbed him from behind and…and…slit his throat." The tears spilled down her cheeks.

"Oh, my God, Jasmine." Olivia hugged her sister tighter. "Did you call the police?"

Her sister nodded. "I did. When I told them what I'd seen, they checked for video footage. The cameras had been turned off. I was the only witness to the murder. Once they realized that, they put me in witness protection and stashed me at a safe house."

Olivia leaned back, her heart hammering. "When did this happen?"

"Two weeks ago."

And she hadn't bothered to call her sister during those two weeks to even know something was wrong. "Oh, Jasmine. I'm so sorry. I should have called you sooner."

"You wouldn't have been able to get me. I had to give up my cell phone, my job, my apartment. Everything. The marshals didn't even give me a chance to go back and collect my own clothes. I've been in witness protection since. Until yesterday."

"I don't understand." Olivia shook her head. "Why didn't they arrest Nico?"

"They did."

"Then why did they put you in witness protection?"

Her sister's mouth twisted. "You don't know who Nico Salvatore is, do you?"

Olivia's brow furrowed. "Should I know that name?"

"I only know it because he and his father have been patrons at the gallery where I work… *worked*." She swallowed hard, more tears slipping down her face. "Vincenzo Salvatore. He's a very rich Italian American with links to the Sicilian mafia. If being the son of a mafia kingpin wasn't bad enough, Nico killed the nephew of Giovanni Romano. He's just as rich and powerful as Nico. Either man could pay anyone enough to silence a witness to any crime."

"Holy smokes, Jaz." Olivia stared into her sister's face. "But the US Marshals had you at a safe house. It should have been…safe."

Jasmine shook her head. "Compromised. Apparently, the Salvatores have connections. Thankfully, the place had an underground tunnel leading into the basement of a neighboring store. While the marshals held off the attack, I escaped through the tunnel and ran. I didn't stop running until I got here."

"You didn't run all the way from Dallas. How did you get here?" Olivia asked.

"I made my way to a truck stop and hitched a ride."

"Jeez." Olivia pressed a hand to her chest. "Hitching a ride could have gotten you killed."

Jasmine snorted. "*Either way*, I could have gotten killed. I hated leaving the marshals to their fate. The cartel hit the safe house with automatic weapons. I can't imagine anyone coming out of that alive."

"Oh, no," Olivia whispered.

"I came to the only place I knew. Home." Her fingers gripped Olivia's arms. "I need money and some clothes. And hair dye, if you have any."

Olivia frowned. "I can give you money and clothes, but you can't run forever."

Jasmine buried her face in her hands, her shoulders shaking with her sobs. "I need to hide... At least until they convict the killer. Maybe even...longer."

Olivia stroked her sister's back. "Sweetie, that's insane."

"I know." She raised her head. "I can't go back to work. I can't have a career. The US Marshals weren't able to keep me safe." She flung her hands in the air. "I don't know what to do." Jasmine stared into her sister's eyes. "But I have to leave as soon as possible. My being here places *you* in danger."

A chill slithered across Olivia's skin. "This will be the first place they look."

Jasmine pushed to her feet, crouching low. "I have to get out of here."

Olivia rose. "Not without me."

"No, Olivia, this is my problem. I can't let you get dragged into it."

"I'm already in it," Olivia said. "You're my only sister. My only family. I can't let you leave without me."

Jasmine hurried down the hallway toward her bedroom. "Do you still have my old clothes?"

"They're right where you left them three years ago."

"I'll need a suitcase." Jasmine quickly closed the blinds and drew the curtains. Then she rummaged through the closet, throwing jeans, shirts and shoes into a pile on the quilt-covered iron bed she'd slept in as a child.

Olivia pulled a suitcase out of the back of her closet and laid it on the bed. "*We'll* need suitcases," she said. "You are *not* leaving without me. We'll figure this out together." She didn't wait for her sister to respond. Instead, she ran to her bedroom, dressed, grabbed her own suitcase from her closet and started packing, her mind racing.

If the US Marshals couldn't keep her sister safe, the mafia would know where to look next. It was only a matter of time before they came looking for her in her hometown of Whiskey Gulch.

Olivia's hands froze. They didn't need to pack. They needed to leave.

Now.

"Jasmine. You're right." Olivia spun and ran toward her bedroom door. "We need to leave. Forget packing. We can buy what we need wherever we land." All she needed was her purse and her car keys. "Hurry."

"Coming." Jasmine wheeled the suitcase down the hallway, stopping before she reached the living room to button the shirt she'd changed into.

"I'm going to grab my purse, and then we're out of here."

Jasmine's brow wrinkled. "You didn't pack a bag?"

"No. If this mafia group knew where to find you at the safe house, they will know to look here. We need to leave immediately."

On her way through the living room to the kitchen, Olivia grabbed the photograph of herself, Jasmine and their parents. She had just stuffed the picture into her purse, grabbed her keys and was heading for the front door when something crashed through the front of the house. Glass, wood and debris exploded into the room, filling it with dust, making it impossible to see clearly.

Olivia stumbled backward in time to avoid being hit and fell, landing hard on her back, the wind knocked out of her lungs. She rolled over and managed to get up onto her hands and knees, coughing as dust filled her nostrils and lungs. She blinked to clear her eyes and gasped.

A large black SUV stood in the middle of the living room, and the doors swung open. Two men wearing dark ski masks hopped out, their silhouettes shadowy in the fog of dust.

Olivia crawled behind the couch, working her

way toward the other side of the room, where Jasmine had been standing in the hallway.

Shards of glass cut into her palms and through the denim of her jeans, piercing her knees. Biting hard on her tongue to keep from crying out, she continued crawling along behind the couch. She had to get to Jasmine and get her out of there before—

A scream ripped through the air.

The men carried a wiggling, kicking, yelling Jasmine toward the SUV.

Olivia jumped to her feet. "Let go of her!" she yelled. She rolled over the back of the couch and ran after them, leaping onto one man's back.

He released his hold on Jasmine and backhanded Olivia, his knuckles catching her temple. The blow sent her flying backward. She hit the wall and sank, her head swimming, her vision going black.

When she came to, the doors to the SUV had closed and the vehicle was backing out of her living room.

"No!" she screamed. She pushed to her feet and raced out of the house through the hole in the wall. The SUV whipped around and sped away into the dusk.

Olivia ran a few steps after them and stopped. She couldn't catch them on foot. She spun around toward her vehicle. Even if she'd had the keys, it wasn't going anywhere—the tires had been slashed.

She hurried into what was left of the house that had been her home all her life and picked her way through the rubble, searching for her purse in the dust and debris.

When she found the bag, she dug out her cell phone. The screen was cracked, but it still worked. She dialed 911 and waited.

When the dispatcher answered, she had to swallow hard past the lump blocking her vocal cords. "You have to stop them. They kidnapped my sister. Please." Her voice cracked. "Help her."

BECKER WAITED UNTIL six thirty at the diner Olivia had suggested. He'd already had two glasses of water, shredded three napkins and apologized to the waitress for taking his time with the menu. He waited another five minutes before concluding he'd been stood up.

Disappointment had robbed him of his appetite. He tossed a twenty on the table and left without ordering. As he exited the diner, a sheriff's vehicle raced past him, strobes flashing and sirens wailing, followed by a fire truck and an ambulance.

He sighed. Someone else was having it worse than he was. Being ditched was lousy; needing

first responders was worse. Becker hoped whoever was in trouble would be all right. Though
Olivia had chosen not to show for their dinner
date, Becker wasn't going to give up. He just
had to try harder.

Olivia was the first person he'd met in Whiskey Gulch. Being new in town, he could use
all the friends he could get. It wasn't like he
was going to marry her. He'd given up on that
institution a long time ago. But he liked company, and he liked her green eyes and shiny
black hair—and that she didn't mind getting
her hands dirty.

A grin tugged at the corners of his mouth.
Since he wasn't going to have dinner with her,
he might see if his new boss was up to meeting
with him that night instead of in the morning.

He pulled out his cell phone and dialed
Trace's number.

Trace answered on the first ring. "Becker!
You made it to Whiskey Gulch?"

"I did," he answered.

"Get on out to the ranch. I'm grilling steaks,
and Mom and Lily are putting all the fixins on
the table. Everything should be ready by the
time you get here."

"I don't want to intrude on your family meal,"
Becker said.

"You're not intruding. As it is, you can meet

the other members of the Outriders. They're all here. When I mentioned steaks and beer, they came running."

Becker laughed. "Can't blame them, can you?"

"They know Whiskey Gulch Ranch beef is the best. Should only take you fifteen minutes to get here from town. We'll be looking for you."

"I'll be there." Becker ended the call and climbed into his truck.

A sheriff's SUV raced by—this time, in the opposite direction—lights flashing, siren wailing.

"Wonder what's going on," he muttered, checking all directions before he pulled out onto the main street running through Whiskey Gulch.

He slowed as he neared Olivia's pottery shop. Had she gotten caught up in her work and forgotten what time it was?

The lights were out, and the Closed sign hung in the window.

As he passed the shop, his cell phone rang. He fished it out of the cupholder and glanced down at a number he didn't recognize. Usually, he would ignore unknown callers, as most were call centers trying to sell him extended warranties on his vehicle or siding on the house he didn't own. But on the off chance it could be Olivia, he answered.

"Hello?"

"Becker?" Olivia's voice sounded in his ear.

Becker pulled into the parking lot of her shop. "Olivia?"

For a moment, she didn't respond.

He could swear he heard a sob, and then her voice came on again, shaky and not at all normal. "I need your help."

He clutched the phone tighter in his hand. "Sweetheart, are you okay?"

"No. I'm not okay." There was no mistaking the sob this time; she was crying.

"Are you safe?"

She let out a bark of laughter that didn't ring true. "I guess."

"Where are you?"

She gave him an address, followed by, "I'm sorry I missed our dinner, but it couldn't be helped."

"I'm on my way. Stay on the phone with me." He entered the address on his map application, turned the truck around and headed away from Whiskey Gulch Ranch and toward the other end of town. "Do I need to call an ambulance?"

"No. They're here."

His heart plummeted to the pit of his belly. "Are they taking care of you?" he asked.

"They tried. But they can't help me. That's why I called you."

As he turned at the last road before leaving town, he could see the sheriff's vehicle, fire truck and ambulance even before he reached her house.

His foot hit the accelerator hard, sending him shooting toward the scene of whatever disaster had befallen Olivia. When he neared the emergency vehicles, he slowed to a stop, shifted into Park and dropped down out of the truck. The GPS map had brought him to a house that appeared as if an armored tank had rammed through the middle, making a huge hole ringed in splintered wood and siding. The roof dipped low in the middle, the support beams destroyed.

Sheriff's deputies stood around with firefighters and EMTs, staring at the damage. In the middle of them was Olivia, her dark hair gray with dust, her hands covered in bandages and the knees of her jeans stained a dark red, almost black, from blood.

Becker's pulse raced, and he broke out in a sweat. The last time he'd seen blood… He shook his head. This wasn't a helicopter crash in Afghanistan—though the house appeared to have been the victim of a crash of some sort.

He breathed in and out several times, a technique he'd learned from the psych doctor he'd been forced to visit for six weeks upon his return from deployment. When his heart slowed enough and he felt more in control, he stepped forward.

His movement caught Olivia's attention, and she looked up.

As soon as she saw him, her tearful eyes grew large and her face crumpled.

Becker opened his arms, and Olivia fell into them, pressing her cheek against his chest.

"What happened?" he asked, his tone calm despite the full-on panic attack that had threatened to overwhelm him only moments before. He wrapped his arms around her and stroked the back of her head in a slow, calming motion.

For a long moment, she didn't speak.

The sheriff's deputy filled him in. "From what Ms. Swann reported, a large black SUV plowed into her home. Men jumped out, grabbed her sister and left."

"Your sister?" Becker tipped her chin up and stared into her watery, red-rimmed green eyes.

Olivia nodded, more tears streaming down her face. "They took her. Oh, dear God. They have my sister."

"Do you know who they were?" Becker cupped her cheek in one hand, brushing away the tears. "Can you describe them?"

Olivia shook her head. "I think they wore ski

masks, and they were covered in dust. When I tried to stop one of them, he slammed me against the wall. I must have blacked out for a second, because when I came to, the SUV was already backing out."

Becker frowned down at her, studying her face through the coating of dust. A bruise was forming on her right temple. "Did you have the EMT check you for potential concussion?"

One of the EMTs leaned into the conversation. "I did. She appears to be okay, but it wouldn't hurt to keep an eye on her. She refused to go to the hospital for a night of observation."

He brushed his thumb gently across the bruise. "If you blacked out—"

Olivia grabbed his hand and captured his gaze with her green-eyed one. "They took my sister. I'm not going anywhere unless it's to find her."

Becker's glance shifted to the deputy.

"We have an all-points bulletin out for a dark SUV with a damaged front end. Dispatch was going to pass that information on to the state police to be on the lookout for it as well."

"It might already be too late," Olivia said. "The people who are after her are only after one thing."

"And what's that?" Becker asked.

"She witnessed a murder." She stared up at

him, her voice shaking as she added, "A dead witness can't testify."

"We passed information about your sister witnessing a murder on to the state police and the feds," the deputy said. "They'll start an investigation to find the people responsible."

"In the meantime, they're getting farther and farther away." She took Becker's hands in hers. "Please, help me find my sister."

"The authorities are doing their best."

She shook her head. "You're going to work for Trace Travis. He has a security firm. I'll hire you. I'll hire all of his team. I'll do anything to get my sister back. Alive." Her fingers squeezed his. "Please. She's the only family I have left."

Becker nodded. "I can't speak for Trace, but I can for myself. I'll do whatever I can to help you. And I'll bet Trace will too." He gathered her to his side and turned to the deputy. "Are you done with Ms. Swann?"

"Yes, sir." He handed Olivia his business card. "If you think of anything else, let us know. Even the smallest detail can be helpful."

"You can't stay here," Becker said.

"I have nowhere else to go," she said. "This was my home."

"You're coming with me." Becker herded Olivia to his truck, helped her into the passenger seat and secured her seat belt. He quickly rounded the front of the vehicle to climb into the driver's seat.

"Where are we going?" she asked.

"To get the help we need." He turned the truck around. "We're going to talk to the leader of the Outriders—my friend and former brother in arms Trace Travis."

Chapter Three

"You knew Trace Travis before he hired you?" Olivia asked as the truck passed through town.

Darkness had settled over Whiskey Gulch, and the stars illuminated the Texas landscape, casting the trees, bushes and hills in a deep indigo blue.

"Trace Travis and I served together as Delta Force operators." Becker's focus remained on the road in front of him. "He's saved my life a number of times, and I've had his back as well."

"He's brought a few of his old army buddies to Whiskey Gulch, hasn't he?"

Becker nodded. "Irish and Levi were members of our team. I'm sure as others leave active duty, they'll come as well."

"Are you all that close?"

"We're closer than blood brothers," he said. "And working for Trace's Outriders, we can use some of the skills we learned as Deltas."

"What exactly does his security firm do?"

Olivia studied the man beside her, desperate for anything to keep her mind off what could be happening to Jasmine.

"Provide protection and investigative extraction services when the authorities are short-handed or their hands are tied. Or the mission is out of their jurisdiction."

Olivia frowned. "Are you some kind of vigilante group?"

Becker shrugged. "We don't break laws, if that's what you're asking. At least, not if we can help it."

Her jaw hardened as she stared out into the darkness. "Frankly, I don't care if you do break a few laws, as long as we get my sister back alive."

"I believe Trace's father had connections here in Texas and with the feds. Hopefully, Trace can encourage those connections to get the ball rolling."

"I hope so." She couldn't imagine what Jasmine was dealing with and didn't want to. She had to be optimistic and do everything in her power to find her.

Becker turned off the highway and pulled up to a gate with the words *Whiskey Gulch Ranch* across a wrought iron arch.

He leaned out his open window and pressed the call button on the keypad.

"That you, Beck?" Trace's voice called out.

"Yes, sir," Becker answered.

"Get up here, man. Steaks are getting cold."

A loud click sounded, and the gate swung open.

Becker drove on and followed the winding road through a stand of oak trees. As they emerged, the lights from the ranch house came into view.

He parked at the side of the house, got out and helped Olivia down from her seat.

They climbed the steps to the long wraparound porch, and a petite woman with blond hair and blue eyes walked out and greeted them on the front porch. "You must be Beck." She held out her hand. "Everyone is gathered in the dining room. I'm Lily, Trace's fiancée."

Becker took her hand. "Lily, pleased to finally meet you. Trace has nothing but good things to say about you."

She smiled. "He's had nothing but good things to say about you as well." When she turned to Olivia, her brows dipped. "Good Lord, Olivia, what happened to you?"

Olivia grimaced. "It's a long story." She knew Lily and Trace from way back when they were kids, growing up in Whiskey Gulch.

"One I'm anxious to hear." Lily hugged her. "Come in. I'm sure Trace will want to hear it as well. No need to tell it more than once to this group."

She hooked her arm around Olivia's elbow and led her through the living area and into the dining room, where there was a long table with seating for up to fourteen people.

The men and women standing around the table turned toward them as they entered.

Trace's mother, Rosalyn Travis, had just set a basket full of bread rolls on the table when she looked up and gasped. "Olivia! What happened?" She hurried forward and touched her bandaged hands. "Come in and sit."

"I'm okay," Olivia said. "Really. I'm sure I can remove these bandages now that the bleeding has stopped."

"*Bleeding?* Good Lord, look at your jeans." Rosalyn's gaze swept over her. "Honey, let's get you cleaned up. You can tell us all about it when we get back to the table."

Olivia let the older woman lead her out of the dining room, thankful for the reprieve. "I'm sorry to show up to your house when I'm such a mess."

"Don't you worry. We'll have you fixed up in no time." Over her shoulder, she called out, "Don't wait on us. Eat while it's hot."

Rosalyn led her up the stairs and straight to the master bedroom, where she rummaged through her closet and pulled out a pair of jeans and a lightweight calf-length sundress in a soft blue floral print. "Which would you prefer?"

"If it's all the same to you, my knees are scraped up from the glass. The dress won't rub against them."

"The dress it is." She put the jeans back and dug in a drawer in her dresser. "My husband gave me this bra-and-panty set before he died, and I haven't had the heart to wear them. I think they will fit you. We're almost the same size."

Olivia shook her head. "I couldn't. He gave them to you. I was so sorry about his death. Your husband was loved by so many in Whiskey Gulch. He helped so many people. Myself included."

Rosalyn smiled and held out the offering of undergarments. "Please. He would have wanted you to have these. He'd understand. That was who he was."

Olivia accepted. "Thank you."

Rosalyn led the way into the spacious bathroom, switched on the shower faucet and adjusted the temperature. "The towels are fresh. There's shampoo, conditioner and bodywash. There's a brush in the top drawer. Help yourself to anything you might need. I'll be downstairs with the others. Take your time. I can warm your supper when you're done."

Olivia's eyes filled at the woman's touching welcome. "Thank you, Mrs. Travis."

"Please, call me Rosalyn. And don't you worry. Everything will work out."

"I hope so," Olivia whispered as the matriarch left the bathroom, closing the door behind her.

For the first time since the SUV had come crashing through her house, Olivia looked at her reflection in the mirror and gasped.

A thin coat of dust covered every inch of her body and made her black hair appear gray. She stripped out of the torn and bloody clothes, the contaminants dirtying the shiny white tiles. She spread a towel on the floor, wrapped her dirty clothes in it and set it aside to take to the laundry room when she was done.

She stepped into the walk-in shower and let the water wash the dust and debris from her hair and scalp. Using a generous amount of shampoo, she quickly washed and rinsed. Afterward, she lathered a washcloth with liquid soap and scrubbed all her nooks and crannies until the water ran clear.

Though she felt better, she couldn't help thinking about Jasmine, frustrated that she was getting clean when she had no idea what was happening to her sister.

A hard knot of guilt formed in her belly as

she dried, dressed and found the brush in the top drawer.

Moments later, she was clean, her hair straightened and pulled back from her forehead. Anxious to get downstairs and see what Trace Travis and the Outriders could do to find her sister, she didn't take the additional time to dry her hair.

The undergarments and the dress fit a little loose but were close enough. Olivia could only feel grateful for the clothing Rosalyn had provided.

Feeling a little more in control of her emotions, Olivia gathered the dirty clothes wrapped in the towel and carried them down the stairs.

Lily met her at the bottom. "I'll take those," she said with a smile. "Please, join the others. They're waiting to hear about what happened. We need to know, in order to help you."

"Thank you." Olivia lifted her chin and marched into the dining room, determined not to shed another tear. Crying accomplished nothing. To find her sister, she needed action.

WHEN OLIVIA WALKED into the dining room wearing the blue dress—her hair slicked back from her forehead, her head held high—Becker had to catch his breath.

The woman had just experienced a traumatic

event, yet she stood before him like a Valkyrie ready to charge into battle.

Still, she was magnificent, strong and beautiful.

He rose from his seat and held out the chair beside him.

When she sank into the chair, he leaned close. "I told them they would have to wait for you to come down until we went into what happened. They're champing at the bit. Do you want to tell them, or should I?"

She gave him a smile. "Please, I'd like you to tell them." Marching in with her head held high was one thing. Retelling the story of her sister's abduction would destroy any confidence she might have built up in the shower.

Becker passed a platter of steak toward her.

"No, thank you," she said. "I'm not hungry."

"Take your time, Olivia," Trace said. "At least drink something. I'm sure this is all difficult for you. We can start by introducing you to the team." He nodded toward Lily. "You've met my better half, Lily."

Lily winked. "We've met."

Lily was petite and spunky. Becker liked that Trace had a woman who could stand on her own. "Trace speaks highly of you, Lily. He said you could face down cowboys twice your size without batting an eyelash."

She lifted her chin. "The key is to never show fear."

Trace chuckled. "I don't think there's anything Lily is afraid of."

Lily leaned against Trace's shoulder. "There is one thing…" Her gaze met his. "Losing you again."

"Baby, I'm not going anywhere," Trace said. "You're stuck with me."

"I can live with that." She smiled up into his eyes.

Becker's heart contracted in his chest. When he was younger, he'd always imagined himself married to someone who would look at him the way Lily looked at Trace. For a brief time, he thought he'd found that person in Brittany. Until Brittany stood him up at the altar and ran off with an accountant. She'd claimed she couldn't handle that he would be gone all the time, doing dangerous things that could get him killed.

He'd been up-front about his work in the army. Apparently, she'd expected him to give it up for her and settle into a low-risk admin job.

The thought of spending his day behind a desk gave him hives.

Trace nodded toward the man to his right. "Beck and Olivia, this is my brother, Matt Hennessey."

"*Half* brother," Matt corrected.

Olivia's brow puckered. "I sense a story behind that."

Trace nodded. "A story for another time. Anyway, Matt's my brother and part of the Outrider team. He had prior service... Marine Force Recon. But we won't hold that against him."

Matt glared at him. "Jealous because you were a lowly Delta?"

Trace grinned once more. "Matt's woman, Aubrey, isn't here tonight."

"She's a home health-care nurse," Matt said. "One of her patients needed some help this evening."

"Moving right along—" Trace nodded toward the familiar face of a man with black hair and blue eyes "—Joseph Monahan, one of my former teammates from the army."

"They call me Irish," he said. "Nice to meet you, Olivia. And it's good to have Beck around again."

Becker nodded. "Good to be with people I know."

"On Irish's other side is his significant other, Tessa Bolton," Trace continued. "An angel of mercy amongst us."

Tessa grimaced. "I'm no angel. But I am a nurse at the local hospital."

Trace smiled at the older woman seated at the

table. "You've met my mother, Rosalyn Travis. She's the glue that holds us all together."

His mother's cheeks filled with a soft shade of pink. "He'd be just fine without me. Lily could handle everything without me around."

Irish leaned toward Tessa and muttered, "Note she didn't say Trace could handle everything."

Trace held up his hands. "I've been gone fighting wars in foreign countries. Before that, my father had a tight fist on how he wanted this ranch run. Since his death, my mother and Lily have been picking up the pieces. They are fully capable of running the ranch operations without my help, giving me the time to pursue my vision for the Outriders."

Trace turned to the last two people at the table. "Levi Warren, also a former Delta from our team."

Levi held up a hand in a short wave. "Nice to meet you. Glad you're with us, Beck. We missed your ugly mug." He winked and cracked half a smile.

"Back atcha, Levi." Becker tipped his head toward the woman seated beside his former teammate. "Who have you got with you?"

Levi grinned and stared down at the woman with sandy-blond hair and gray eyes. "She's only the smartest, prettiest badass in the county sheriff's department. Deputy Dallas Jones, my fiancée."

"Now that all the introductions are out of the way…" Trace looked around the room. "I trust everyone is up to speed on the abduction of Olivia's sister?"

As one, each person at the table nodded.

Dallas leaned toward Olivia. "I got a call about the BOLO they put out on the black SUV. I'm sorry about your sister."

Even as Olivia's eyes welled, she squared her shoulders. "We'll get her back."

Becker only hoped they would get Jasmine back *alive*. He launched into an explanation of what had happened.

"Excuse me," Trace said after Becker had finished. He left the table and returned with a laptop. He opened it and waited for the system to boot.

"Says here, Nico Salvatore's initial court date is a week from today. They will arraign him then. According to the press releases, he's pleading not guilty. They have no evidence. The murder weapon is still missing, and his girlfriend claims he was with her at the time of the murder."

"He was if she was also at the scene of the crime." Olivia shook her head. "My sister *was* there. If she said it was Nico, it was Nico. She has no reason to lie. Jasmine also said Eduardo was carrying what appeared to be a painting. She didn't have time or access to determine which painting he was carrying. Nico took it from Eduardo and left."

In between bites of his steak, Trace's fingers flew across the keyboard. "I found a report on a missing painting from the Cavendish Art Gallery in downtown Dallas."

Olivia's eyes widened. "That's the gallery my sister curated."

"The report says the police have no suspects at this time, citing faulty or disarmed security cameras. They do mention the curator, a Miss Jasmine Swann, is missing. By stating the curator has gone missing, the reporter is leaving it to the readers to infer Ms. Swann might be the one who stole the painting."

"But she didn't," Olivia cried. "Nico did."

Trace toggled back and forth between articles. "Nico was arrested the following morning. That gave him time to hide or dispose of the painting."

Irish speared a piece of his steak. "With Nico's life hanging in the balance, Salvatore would have every reason to want your sister dead. I'm sure his father does not want his son rotting in jail." He popped the steak in his mouth and chewed.

Becker's eyes narrowed. "If all Salvatore wanted was to keep his son out of jail, why didn't he have his people kill Jasmine instead of taking her hostage?"

Olivia stiffened next to him. "Unless it wasn't Salvatore who kidnapped my sister."

Becker turned to her. "Who else?"

"Eduardo Romano's family," Levi said. "They have reason to want Jasmine to testify. That way, Nico would pay for his crime. Texas has the death penalty."

Trace glanced up. "The other question is, what happened to the painting?"

"If Eduardo had it initially, do you think the Romanos want it back?" Lily asked. "Could they be the ones who actually kidnapped Jasmine? I mean, they didn't kill her. They obviously wanted her alive, or why not just burn the house down with her in it? Or shoot her?"

Becker reached under the table to grip Olivia's hand. Her fingers curled between his.

"Do you think they might want to bargain with the Salvatores?" Tessa said. "The witness for the painting?"

"What was so special about the painting that Nico would kill to get it?" Levi asked.

Trace tapped his fingers against the keyboard a few times and turned the laptop around so that everyone could see the image on the screen.

A woman stood with her back to the artist in a field of wheat, her long dark hair whipped by the wind, her body naked, blending naturally in the late-afternoon light of a fading sun.

"She's beautiful," Rosalyn whispered. "It's like something Andrew Wyeth would have done."

Trace nodded. "That's because it is. It was commissioned by one of Wyeth's patrons. The man had Wyeth paint this portrait of his wife. The patron has since passed. The wife and her family wanted the work displayed for all to see before they sold it to the highest bidder."

"Wow. No wonder both mafia families want it," Olivia said. "It's an original Wyeth."

"But why display it at the Cavendish Art Gallery?" Becker asked.

"Good point," Tessa said. "Wouldn't it have been better to place it with other paintings from Wyeth's collection?"

Olivia shook her head. "Wyeth's paintings could be on tour from one gallery to another around the world. The family might not want the painting that far away. Art enthusiasts who love Wyeth would come to see this newly discovered treasure."

"Some would pay big bucks to own it," Trace said. "An Andrew Wyeth painting could sell for millions."

"All the more reason to steal it," Dallas said. "They're going to sell it on the black market."

"They might already have a buyer lined up," Becker said.

Trace's lips twisted. "I bet both families had the same idea. They might both have a buyer—maybe even the money already in their hands."

"Then that's all the incentive they need to snag the painting," Olivia said. "Even if they have to kill someone to get it." She squeezed Becker's hand beneath the table. "Jasmine has to be okay. They kidnapped her for a reason, and it wasn't to kill her. They're going to use her as a bargaining chip."

"I've read there are auctions set up specifically for black market items," Dallas said. "Seems they could get a bigger payoff if more than one person is bidding on the painting."

Olivia's brow furrowed. "Hopefully, they haven't delivered the painting to a buyer yet. It's been a couple of weeks since it went missing."

"If Nico was smart," Becker said, "he hid it and didn't tell anyone where it is. All the more reason for his entire family to want to get the murder charges dropped and Nico out of jail in a hurry."

Trace closed the laptop and set it on a buffet table behind him. "We have a lot to think about.

It makes sense to keep Jasmine alive if she's to be used as leverage for the painting."

"We need to locate the painting," Olivia said. "We could use it in trade for my sister's life."

"Not if you turn it over to the police," Dallas said.

Becker stared at the sheriff's deputy. "Are you saying we should withhold evidence?"

She held up her hands. "I wouldn't exactly put it in those terms. But once that painting is back where it belongs, you won't have anything to bargain with."

"She's right," Olivia said. "We might have to be just as crooked as the mafia long enough to get my sister out of trouble."

Dallas covered her ears. "This is where I have to step out of the discussion. I made an oath to uphold the law. But what I don't know, I can't report."

"Let's table this discussion until after dinner," Rosalyn said. "Please, eat. And when we're done here, I have pecan pie for dessert."

Becker finished his steak, all the while his thoughts churning, a plan forming. His idea might be way off base, but it was just crazy enough that it might work. He glanced over at Olivia, knowing she would want to be in on the plan. The hard part was that this plan, if they chose to go with it, would place both of them in danger and right in the middle of rival mafia families.

But if it worked, they stood a chance of snagging the painting and getting Jasmine back alive.

He was up for the challenge. His training as a Delta had given him the fighting skills he would need if he was backed into a corner.

Olivia, on the other hand, wasn't a fighter. She was an artist. She'd be in way over her head.

But if he didn't take her with him, she'd find a way to follow and get herself into all kinds of trouble anyway. If she insisted, he'd be better off knowing she was by his side rather than off by herself, a loose cannon on a rocking ship.

Becker polished off the last bite of his food and waited impatiently for the others to finish. When Rosalyn rose from the table, he rose too, helped clear the dishes and carried them into the kitchen.

"Rosalyn, Trace—" Dallas set her plate in the sink "—thank you for dinner. I'll just see myself to the door so your team can make plans I might not want to know about." She leaned forward and brushed a kiss across Rosalyn's cheek. "Keep them somewhat in line, will you? I don't want to put any of my people in jail if I can help it."

Rosalyn patted Dallas's cheek. "You haven't always played by the rules, my dear."

"Good point. But I did that out of self-preservation." She turned to Trace. "I might be stepping out of this conversation, but I'm around if you need me. I'll always have your back. After all, you had mine when I needed the help." She reached for Levi's hand. "And you have my back."

"Always, darlin'. Always." He walked her out.

Once they were out of the house, Becker met Trace's gaze. "I have an idea."

Trace nodded. "Let's help with the cleanup. Then we can take it to my office."

"Normally, I'd make you stay and help," Lily said. "But Olivia needs you more." She pushed up on her toes and pressed a kiss to Trace's lips. "We've got this. Go."

"Thank you." Trace led the way through the door. "I believe we have your first assignment as an Outrider agent."

Becker nodded. He hadn't been sure what to expect. Playing the bodyguard or providing security at events, yeah. But going undercover with the mafia hadn't even been a passing thought.

Chapter Four

Olivia followed Becker as they walked down a hallway to a set of wood-paneled doors.

Trace opened them to reveal a large office with a massive desk at one end and a conference table at the other. He waved toward the table. "Have a seat."

Becker pulled out a chair for Olivia.

She didn't really feel like sitting. Her natural inclination was to pace. But she didn't want to argue, so she took the proffered seat and waited to hear what Becker had to say, praying his idea was sound and would lead to them getting Jasmine back safe and sound.

Matt, Irish and Levi took seats around the table. Trace closed the doors and sank into the chair at the end of the long table. "What have you got?"

"I understand you have connections," Becker said. "Do you happen to have any in the dark web?"

Trace frowned. "Maybe. Why?"

Becker's jaw hardened. "We need to gather all the information we can get about the Salvatores and the Romanos. We also need to find out who else has enough money and interest in art to purchase a stolen Andrew Wyeth—someone I can impersonate."

"That's a lot to ask." Trace leaned back in his chair.

"I might be able to help you with the dark web," Matt said. "My mother helped a young hacker once when he was cornered by some mean rednecks. Saved his life. I'm sure he'd want to return the favor."

Becker nodded. "Tap into that resource. Look for an auction that might be selling stolen art. I'll need as much of that information as I can get. In the meantime, I'll need to craft my new identity with a driver's license, credit cards, clothes and an expensive sports car."

Trace laughed. "This kind of thing takes time."

"We don't have a lot of time," Olivia said.

Trace sobered. "Of course," he assured her. "We'll make it happen."

"And while your hacker is at it," Olivia said, "make sure he gets information on what your rich art-loving sleazebag likes in the way of women." She shot a glance at Becker. "If you're going undercover, I'm going with you."

He took her hands. "You realize we'll be dancing with dangerous people?"

She nodded. "Been there. You saw my house. Besides, we're talking about saving my sister. I refuse to stand by and do nothing."

"They might recognize you," he said. "You have pretty distinctive features."

She lifted her chin. "I can change my appearance. We both have to do something to impersonate whomever the hacker can find."

Matt shifted in his seat. "How soon do you need this information?"

"The sooner, the better," Olivia answered. "My sister might not have much time."

"We'll also need you to have the hacker spread the word that we are in the market for an Andrew Wyeth painting and will pay top dollar." Becker tapped his fingertips on the tabletop.

Matt grabbed a pad of paper and a pen from the middle of the table and jotted down notes. "Should we spread other rumors about more potential buyers?"

"Yes," Becker said. "Hopefully, they'll be greedy enough to want a bidding war. Maybe they'll arrange for an in-person auction." He glanced at Olivia. "We'll want an invite to that."

"It all sounds too fantastic." Her brow knit. "Can we pull off something this complicated?"

Becker nodded. "We have to lure the two factions out in the open."

"In the meantime, Matt, Irish and I will be searching for Jasmine," Trace said. "If we find her first, we can save you the trouble of all the pretense."

Becker nodded.

If only it was that easy. Olivia feared it wouldn't end that quickly. "As long as the Romanos think Jasmine is of value, and they don't have the painting, they'll come after her again."

Becker drew in a deep breath and released it slowly. "Then we return the painting to the rightful owners."

"That will help with the Romanos but not the Salvatores," Olivia said. "Until Nico is locked up for good, Jasmine will remain a target."

"Then once we find her, we'll get her to a safe location."

"Can you guarantee her safety?" Olivia asked. "The US Marshals couldn't."

Trace's brow dipped. "You have my word. I can assign one of my men to protect her."

"For how long? Weeks? Months? Years?" Olivia shook her head. "You can't commit to that kind of long-term protection."

"Wanna bet?" He leaned toward her. "Let's get her back and take it from there."

Olivia forced herself to breathe normally. She

couldn't freak out now; Jasmine needed her to keep a calm, cool head. Especially if she was going incognito in order to rescue her.

Trace glanced at Matt, who was scribbling notes on the pad. His eyes narrowed. "This hacker you know… Do you trust him?"

Matt looked up. "With my life."

Trace's lips quirked. "I wouldn't happen to know him, would I?"

Matt's mouth twitched. He held Trace's gaze for a long moment in silence.

Olivia studied the two men as they communicated without saying anything.

Trace nodded. "Enough said."

She almost laughed. If she'd read their looks right, Matt Hennessey not only trusted the hacker—he *was* the hacker.

The knowledge made her feel a little better. At least they were keeping this operation within the team. A random hacker might be up for sale.

Olivia glanced around the room at the men who'd worked, fought and would lay down their lives for each other. She was in good hands. If anyone could find and rescue her sister, it was these stalwart men.

Her heart warmed as she sat beside Becker, glad he'd walked into her shop that afternoon.

He was different from other men she'd known. Becker was nothing like her former fiancé. Mike would never have put himself in danger for anyone. He would have walked the other way. Not Becker. The man was planning to put himself in harm's way for her, a veritable stranger.

Like he had done earlier, she reached beneath the table for his hand and gave it a gentle squeeze.

His lips turned upward, and he responded in kind.

"Are you sure you want to do this?" he asked. "You don't have to. I can handle this operation on my own. I'd feel better if I did."

She shook her head. "And who would have your back?"

"Trace or Irish."

Both men nodded.

Olivia shook her head. "It would look more natural for the rich guy to bring his girlfriend. He'd want to impress her with the money."

"She has a point," Irish said. "They might be more open to you if you have a woman with you rather than a couple of bodyguards."

Trace tipped his head. "Although, we could be your bodyguards even if you take Olivia in with you. A rich man would travel with them. He'd be a target for kidnapping and ransom."

"We'll play it by ear," Becker said. "Let's get our stories down, hijack the identity of a man who's most likely to purchase a stolen painting and see what happens then."

"On it." Matt pushed to his feet. "I'll have my contact get to work. Hopefully, we'll have something by morning."

Olivia met Matt's gaze. "Thank you." She turned to the others in the room. "I appreciate what you're doing for my sister." For the first time since she'd found her sister cowering in her kitchen, Olivia was optimistic.

Trace nodded. "We'll do our best. In the meantime, I'll send my foreman over to your place tomorrow and see what he can do to mitigate the damage and weatherproof it until we can get a carpenter to repair the structure."

Her heart swelled and tears sprang to her eyes. "I don't know what I would have done if Becker hadn't shown up in my shop today."

Trace's brow wrinkled. "I don't know what that has to do with us helping."

She smiled through the liquid swimming in her eyes. "It brought me to all of you."

"My mother will probably have a room ready for you. You're welcome to stay with us as long as you like. It will take time to repair your home. You can go with the foreman tomorrow and gather some of your belongings and bring them here."

Olivia swallowed the lump in her throat. "Thank you."

They left the room and returned to the kitchen, where Rosalyn, Lily and Tessa sat around the kitchen table, drinking coffee.

Rosalyn popped out of her seat. "There you are. Did you find a way to save the world? Or at the very least, Olivia's sister?"

"We're working on it," Trace said.

"Well, while you're working on it, let me show our guest to her room. I'm sure all the trauma of the day has taken its toll." She hooked her arm through Olivia's. "Let me show you where you'll sleep for the next few weeks."

"I could sleep over my shop in town," Olivia insisted. "There's a storage room I could convert into sleeping quarters."

"Is there a bed?"

"No. But I could bring one from the house."

"Is there a bathroom with a shower?"

Olivia shook her head, the events of the day hitting her like a ton of bricks. "No. I should just quit arguing and say thank you, shouldn't I?"

Lily laughed. "Yes, ma'am. When Rosalyn Travis gets in mama mode, she won't take no for an answer."

"She's right. And you, my dear, could use a little mothering." She led her out of the kitchen. "I knew your mother. She was a lovely woman and a talented artist. I have one of her paintings. Did you know that?"

Olivia couldn't resist the comfort Mrs. Travis provided. It was almost as good as having her own mother there to tell her everything would be all right.

Rosalyn spoke softly of her friendship with Olivia's mother and the time she took painting lessons from her. "Alas, I didn't have the talent—or was it the patience?—to learn." She shrugged with a smile. "That's when I bought one of her paintings. It's hanging in the room you'll be sleeping in. I figured if I couldn't paint, I should at least help someone be successful at what she did best by purchasing one of her works."

At the top of the stairs, she turned right and led her to a room two doors down. "This is the blue room. It has its own bathroom. You won't have to traipse down the hallway." She pushed the door open.

Olivia's heart swelled when she saw the painting hanging over the white iron bed. Her mother had painted a picture of a white wooden porch overlooking a sandy beach, the blue green of the ocean waves shimmering beyond.

The bed was covered with a seafoam-green comforter and matching pillows.

Rosalyn crossed the room to the French doors

on the other side. "I like to open the window or door at night to let the cool night breeze flow through." She pulled open the doors and walked out onto the porch. "It's a beautiful night. The breeze is so peaceful." She lifted her face to the sky, a slight smile softening her features.

Olivia joined her on the porch and stared up at the night sky, where a blanket of stars stretched in all directions. "It is a beautiful night," she said. "When we were little, my sister and I used to lie outside under the stars with our parents and point out the constellations and make wishes on shooting stars." Olivia chose to remember the good in those memories, not the loss of her parents and the danger her sister faced.

"I used to do that with Trace. He loved learning about the stars and planets. For a while, I thought he'd be an astronaut. But he chose to join the army." She sighed. "I didn't want him to. I was afraid every time he deployed. I didn't want to be one of those parents visited by a man in a fancy uniform, there to tell me my son was coming home in a body bag." Rosalyn turned to her with a crooked smile that faded away. "As it was, my son came home when my husband was murdered. He was safer at war than his father was at home."

Olivia touched the older woman's arm. "I'm so sorry."

Rosalyn covered her hand with her own. "I am too. But life goes on. I'm glad Trace is home, but I hope he didn't stay because of me. I never wanted him to be trapped by this big ol' ranch. Lily and I could have managed." She snorted. "Or we would have gone down fighting."

"I've seen Trace around town. He seems to love what he's doing. He's always got a kind word and a smile."

"Thank you, dear." Rosalyn smiled. "He and his boys will find your sister. Don't you worry. They're good at what they do. Now, I've laid out a nightgown, a robe and slippers. There's a new toothbrush in the bathroom and all the toiletries you might need. If you need anything, please let me know."

"You've done more than enough for me. Thank you." Olivia hugged Rosalyn.

When she left, she closed the door behind her.

Olivia was finally alone in a pretty room with her mother's painting. Her sister was out there somewhere, being held captive by the animals who'd carried her away screaming.

How could she go on?

By putting one foot in front of the other and taking care of herself. She would be of no use to her sister if she didn't get enough rest.

She changed into the pretty, semi-sheer nightgown and lay on the bed.

She was exhausted and weary.

As soon as she closed her eyes, images of the SUV crashing through the wall of her home flashed over and over in her mind like a video on a loop.

She opened her eyes to dispel the images and stared up at the ceiling, following the shadows created by the starlight shining through the windows.

After thirty minutes, she sat up and swung her legs over the side of the bed. Maybe a drink of water would help. She was anxious. After wrapping the robe around the nightgown, she slipped her feet into the soft terry-cloth slippers and padded to the door.

After a quick peek into the hallway, she stepped out and descended the staircase to the first floor.

The lights were off, but several night-lights provided enough illumination. She made it to the kitchen, where someone had left a light on over the sink.

She searched until she found the cabinet with the glasses and filled one with tap water and several cubes of ice.

The thought of going back up the stairs to lie

alone didn't appeal to her, so she walked out the back door and onto the porch.

Rosalyn was right: the cool night breeze was peaceful.

Olivia crept across the porch to the end, where a swing swayed slightly in the gentle breeze. She set the glass on a table and sank onto the cushioned seat with a sigh. Maybe she'd rock herself to sleep.

"That was a deep sigh," a warm, resonant voice said in the darkness. Becker pushed away from the wall of the house, emerging from the shadows.

A tremor of awareness rippled through Olivia. "I thought you had a room in town?"

"I do, but Trace insisted I stay. Saves time if I'm here instead of all the way in town. He and Matt are working in the office. I imagine they'll be there all night."

"And you're not with them?"

"I was for a while, but there were only the two computers. I didn't like crowding them by hanging over their shoulders."

"Matt's the hacker, isn't he?" Olivia grinned. "Why doesn't he just confess?"

"Hacking can get you thrown in jail, and worse, if you break into the wrong systems," Becker said.

"I guess you're right." She drew her fingers

across her lips. "I know nothing about any hacking going on."

"Neither do I."

Olivia scooted to one side of the porch swing. "You can sit. I promise not to bite."

He settled on the cushioned seat beside her and leaned back. "What if I want you to?"

"I'm sure we could work something out," she shot back.

"Why aren't you sleeping?" he asked. "I would think you're pretty tired after what you went through today."

"I am. But I can't get my mind to relax."

He slipped his arm around her shoulders and pulled her close. "If you want me to stay with you until you go to sleep, I can."

"You've already done so much for me," she said and yawned. "But okay. I accept." She leaned her body into his, her cheek resting against his chest.

"That can't be all that comfortable," he said and shifted his body. Turning to the side, he scooped her into his arms and deposited her in his lap, guiding her head onto his shoulder. "Better?"

She melted against him, loving how hard his body was compared to her softer curves and how warm he was in the cool breeze.

His arms wrapped around her, holding her close.

Olivia rested her cheek against his chest, the steady beat of his heart calming the storm of memories rushing through her mind. She inhaled deeply, and on a slow exhalation, she released some of the day's stress.

She'd just met him earlier that day; yet here she was, draped across his lap, dressed in a nightgown and a robe, feeling cherished in his strong arms.

She couldn't help thinking it would be nice to be loved by someone like Becker. The woman he married would be one lucky lady. He would stand by her, protect her, and never destroy the sanctity of their love and trust for one another by hiring a prostitute.

That thought led to another. "Have you ever been married?"

He shook his head. "No."

"How is it that you're still single?" she whispered.

"I came close once," he said, his voice as warm as melted chocolate.

"'Close'? What happened?"

"I showed up. She didn't."

Olivia leaned back and stared into his face. Her heart fluttered. "She stood you up at the altar?"

He grimaced. "I know. My life is a cliché.

I haven't had the desire to repeat the humiliation since."

"She must have been blind and stupid." Olivia shook her head. "I can't believe she didn't show up for her own wedding."

He chuckled. "She realized at the last minute that she couldn't be married to a military man who wouldn't be home for her birthday, Valentine's Day, Christmas. She married an accountant."

Olivia rested her cheek back on his chest. "They deserved each other. She settled for boring when she could have had you."

His laughter rumbled against her ear. "I'll take that as a compliment."

"You should. She wasn't the right woman for you. You dodged a bullet."

He nodded, his hand coming up to stroke her hair. "I know that now, but I can't lie… It hurt when I was standing there, waiting for a bride who never showed up."

"Hurt your pride, most likely." Olivia bit her tongue. "Sorry. I shouldn't have said that. Did you love her?"

He didn't answer at first.

Olivia regretted asking the question. She hadn't intended to put him on the spot or make him uncomfortable.

Finally, he said, "I was young and stupid. I

think I was more in love with the idea of being married. Of having someone to come home to more than having the right someone to spend my life with."

She glanced up at him. "That's pretty profound. Did you realize that at the time?"

He snorted. "I realized it just now." Becker pressed a kiss to her forehead. "It took meeting you for my thoughts to become clear enough to understand why I was so hurt at the time."

"And why was that?" she asked.

"I wanted all of it. Marriage, kids…the love of a good woman." His chest rose and fell beneath her cheek. "I just didn't take the time to find the right person to do all that with. Then I told myself I shouldn't marry. The job makes any relationship too hard. I gave up."

"When you could have found a woman who would have accepted you for who you are and understood that your military service meant so much to you." Her hand rested over his heart. "And now?"

His arms tightened around her. "I think there's hope for the future." Again, he kissed her forehead.

"I'm glad I could help," she said. "Not that I did anything."

"You did everything," he said. "You asked the questions that made me think past my pride.

Thank you." With a grin, he cupped her cheek and kissed her on the lips.

With her hand resting on his chest, it wasn't hard to move it up to circle the back of his neck and deepen the kiss. Olivia made that bold move so naturally, she didn't realize she'd done it until her fingers pushed through his hair.

His tongue swept across the seam of her lips, urging her to open to him.

She did, meeting him thrust for thrust, their tongues entwining in a sensual caress.

Heat surged through her veins, dispelling the coolness of the breeze and sending fire to her core, where it coiled and intensified.

His hand slid down her arm to her waist and lower to smooth over her hip…and lower still, finding the hem of her robe halfway down her thigh.

Yes.

She wanted to feel his hand on her bare skin, riding up beneath the robe and the gown to cup her bottom, pressing her body closer to his.

Beneath her, she could feel the hardness of his erection digging into her other hip. All she had to do was shift her weight, straddle his hips and lower herself over him to consummate the burgeoning desire flooding her system.

It wouldn't be impossible. Tricky, considering the swing. But not impossible.

When she started to move, he broke the kiss and leaned back, dragging in a shaky breath. "I'm sorry. I got a little carried away." He lifted her and sat her on the seat beside him. "If you like, I'll walk you to your room and wait with you while you go to sleep." He raised his hands. "I promise not to take advantage of you. Just be there so you can sleep without bad guys driving into your home."

Inside, Olivia was screaming, *No, no, no!*

They couldn't stop there.

She wanted so much more.

Chapter Five

Still shaking from the intensity of her desire, all Olivia could do was nod.

Becker stood up and held out his hand.

She laid hers in his and rose to her feet. Her slipper slid off her foot, and she fell forward.

Becker caught her and held her longer than was necessary to regain her balance.

Olivia didn't complain. She was back in his arms, loving the feeling of strength and security he imparted.

When he pushed her out to arm's length, the cool air between them felt too empty. She considered propositioning him.

All the way up the stairs, she mentally rehearsed asking him to stay with her, to make love to her and hold her through the night.

When they reached her room, he swept her up into his arms once more and carried her over the threshold, laying her across the bed.

Then he bent to press another kiss to her forehead.

Olivia lifted her face to him, circled her hands behind his head and brought his lips to hers. Forehead kisses were for friends and children. She didn't want to be just his friend. And she wasn't a child. Her heart slamming against her ribs, Olivia kissed him long and hard. All the words she'd rehearsed in her head flew from her mind.

"Stay with me," she whispered against his mouth.

"I shouldn't."

"Why?"

"We just met."

"Bad reason. Try again." She resumed the kiss and pulled him down onto the bed beside her.

He sank down on the mattress, lay on his side and brushed her hair back from her forehead. "I don't want to rush you," he said. "Whatever we're feeling is special. I can't blow it. I want it too badly."

"And so do I," she said softly. "We're not kids."

"No, we're not," he said, sliding his thumb across her jawbone.

Olivia ran her hand over his shoulder and down to the small of his back, applying pressure, reminding him of the hardness digging into her hip. "We're consenting adults."

He brushed a featherlight kiss across first one eyelid and then the other. "Mmm. Yes, we are."

"I'm not asking for forever," she said. "I don't want to be alone tonight. Please." There it was—she was so desperate to be with this man, she had been reduced to begging. She knew no shame, but she didn't care, as long as he stayed.

He paused his onslaught of kisses on her face and lifted his head to stare into her eyes. "If I stay, it won't be just kisses."

"I want more." She took his hand in hers and guided it to the hem of her robe, sliding his fingers beneath the soft silk and then beneath the thin chiffon of the gown beneath.

Her breath caught at the feel of his skin against hers as she moved his hand up over her hip and across her torso to cup one of her breasts. She held him there, her breath ragged as if she couldn't quite get enough air into her lungs.

For a fraction of a second, he hesitated. Then his fingers curled around her, finding the tip and teasing the nipple into a tight little pearl.

Her back arched off the mattress.

More. She wanted so much more.

Becker reached for the belt of her robe, untied it and opened the lapels wide.

The nightgown did little to hide Olivia's attributes. Not that she wanted it to. She wanted to be completely naked with the man. Impatient, she sat up, ripped off the nightgown and flung it against the wall. It slipped softly and soundlessly to the floor.

Olivia lay back against the mattress and slid her hands beneath the hem of his T-shirt, bringing it up and over his head. She tossed it aside, and it landed on top of her gown. He was all muscle and sinew, and she reveled in running her hands over his smooth skin and impressive chest.

The man was magnificent.

When she reached for the button on his jeans, he brushed her hands aside, ripped open the rivet, unzipped and stepped out of the jeans to stand before her in all his glorious masculinity.

She held her breath as he came to her, parted her legs and dropped to his knees.

"I want you inside me," she said. "Now."

He shook his head. "Not yet. I want you to want me as much as I want you right now."

Olivia collapsed back against the mattress with a moan. "I already do."

"I'm here to prove you wrong."

As soon as he parted her folds and touched his tongue to her most sensitive spot, she knew he was right.

Shocks of electricity rippled through her at the first touch. The second flick of his tongue had her sensations pulsing, lighting her nerve endings, making her body sizzle with anticipation.

Olivia dug her hands into his hair, the ecstasy so profound, she didn't know whether to push him away or bring him closer.

She chose closer.

He swirled and flicked and licked her there until her body writhed to the pace he set.

Her hips rocked, rising and falling as she let go of her worry and embraced the moment.

Beautiful tension rose within her, her muscles tightening, her heels digging into the mattress as she savored everything he was doing to her.

Tingling started at her core and spread outward until she was consumed by her release.

She rode the wave for as long as it lasted and then finally collapsed back against the pillow—her breathing coming in shallow gasps, her heartbeat raging.

For a long moment, she lay still, reveling in the afterglow. But only for a moment. They weren't done. Not yet. She wanted to feel him inside her, filling that space that had been empty for too long. Had it ever been filled? Mike hadn't touched her quite as *completely* as Becker had.

This was…different…more intense…so much better. Olivia didn't want it to end.

She sank her fingers into his hair again and pulled.

"Hey," he chuckled. "The hair is attached."

"Now," she managed to say. "I need you now."

"Well, then. Okay." He climbed up her body, settled between her legs, pressed his staff against her channel…and stopped.

Olivia groaned, grabbed his buttocks and tried to bring him home.

He shook his head. "Wait."

"No."

"Trust me, you'll want to wait." He leaned over the side of the bed, grabbed his jeans and dug into the back pocket for his wallet.

It was then that Olivia realized Becker was thinking more clearly than she was. He was right. She was glad he'd waited as he rolled the protection down over his engorged staff.

Then he was back between her legs, nudging her entrance. He leaned up on his arms, staring down into her eyes. "You are a beautiful, amazing and talented woman, Olivia Swann."

She looked up at the gorgeous man—even more beautiful naked than any man had a right to be. "You're pretty talented yourself." Her hands wrapped around his hips, her fingers pressing into the taut skin of his buttocks.

"Make love to me, Becker. Before we forget where we left off."

He laughed. "I have a memory like a—"

Before he could utter another word, she lifted her hips and came down on him, hard and deep.

BECKER HELD ON TO his control by a thread. The woman was so hot, sexy and willing, he wasn't sure how much longer he could hold back. But he did, wanting to make the moment last even longer.

What they were doing—how he was feeling—was pure magic, and he never wanted it to end.

Taking his time, he moved in and out of her. Slowly at first.

Her fingers dug into him again, urging him to pick up the pace.

He complied, the tension mounting inside, his body tensing even more with every thrust and parry.

Her muscles tightened, and she gripped him like a fitted glove, providing slick friction that ignited every part of his soul.

Soon, he was pumping hard and fast, past the point of no return, ready to take her all the way. As he neared the peak, he let go of his restraint, and with one final thrust, he spasmed. He pulsed inside her as wave after wave of ecstasy washed over him, reminding him of how good it felt to make love to someone incredibly special.

Olivia was that someone. He'd known it the moment he'd found her at the back of her shop, her hands gray with wet clay, smudges of it drying on her face. She'd looked up at him with those incredible green eyes, and it was as if he'd been sucker punched in the gut.

He knew he had to see her again. All the years of telling himself he wasn't marriage material, that no woman would or should marry a Delta Force operator, had been his way of pushing women away. He hadn't wanted to risk rejection again.

Until a talented artist, covered in clay and charm, had smiled up at him.

He held his body stiffly, absorbing every bit of his release, relishing the moment in her arms. Olivia was the real deal.

Maybe it was too soon to think about forever, but he was determined not to fail this time. If she really was the one, he'd do everything to win her heart.

As he returned to Earth, he lowered himself onto her and rolled them both to the side, maintaining their intimate connection as long as possible.

He held her close in his arms and pressed his

lips to hers in a gentle kiss he hoped conveyed even a fraction of his joy.

When his heart slowed enough to where he could breathe normally, he asked, "Are you all right?"

Olivia raised her hand to his cheek and smiled. "More than all right." She breathed deeply, her breasts pressing against him.

"You should rest," he said.

She yawned and nodded, closing her eyes. "So should you."

"I will as soon as I know you're sleeping peacefully."

"You'll stay?" she whispered, her hand dropping to rest on his chest.

"I'll stay," he promised. "Now, sleep."

She nestled close, her body pressing against his. Her breathing slowed, and finally, she slept. From what Becker could tell, she wasn't fighting bad guys in her dreams—probably not dreaming at all.

He held her tight. He was almost afraid to sleep. Afraid that when he woke, what had just happened would have all been a dream. He'd be alone in his bed, and Olivia would have been a product of his imagination.

To keep the dream alive, he stayed awake, his gaze on the woman he held, hoping this was the real deal.

For a few short minutes, while making love with Olivia, Becker had pushed aside the mission he'd proposed, focusing instead on this woman and the chemistry between them that neither could deny.

He couldn't do that again. Not until they'd successfully located Jasmine, retrieved the painting and put Nico behind bars permanently. Until then, Jasmine and Olivia were in danger.

His resolve firm, he drifted into half sleep, his awareness not far from the surface. When they woke the next day, they would have work to do. He needed all his faculties operating at 100 percent.

His sleep was plagued by images of Olivia covered in dust, her arms and legs bleeding. He wouldn't let that happen again. Not on his watch. He'd protect her with his life, if that was what it took.

He hoped he wouldn't have to make that decision, because he only had one life to give. Then who would take care of Olivia and make sure she was safe for the rest of her life?

His last thought as he faded into sleep was that he wouldn't let this mission get to the point of sacrificing his life to save another. He had to stay alive to be there for her.

Chapter Six

Becker slept for a few hours and woke as the gray light of dawn edged through the windows.

He lay on his back for a few minutes, enjoying waking beside Olivia, wondering if they'd ever have the opportunity to do it again.

If he had anything to say about it, they would. But first, they had to find Jasmine and the painting. Once they were secure, he could pursue Olivia. How far *she* wanted to go with *him*, he still wasn't sure. For Becker, forever seemed to be floating around in his mind.

Frankly, that scared him. He'd just met her, and he was already thinking about the long term. Was he so in love with the dream of finding a family that he was jumping ahead when he should be taking it slowly?

To keep from waking Olivia, Becker eased out of bed. Once he'd dressed, he slipped from the room and paused when he turned to close the door behind him.

Olivia slept with abandon, her arms splayed out, her cheeks a rosy pink, her dark hair fanned out around her head on the seafoam-green pillows.

His heart tugged at him, urging him to go back to her, lie down in the bed and hold her once more. With the plan he had in mind, he might not get that chance again anytime soon.

Just as he was about to take that step, he heard another door open at the end of the hallway.

To avoid awkwardness for himself and Olivia, he pulled the door closed and hurried to the head of the stairs. As he glanced back, he caught Rosalyn's gaze.

She smiled and nodded, indicating he should continue down the stairs.

He didn't, preferring to wait for his host instead.

She carried a basket full of laundry, which he removed from her hands.

"I can carry it," she insisted.

"I know," he said with a smile of his own. "But my mother taught me to help with all household chores."

"As she should. There is no such thing as women's work or men's work. We all pitch in to get things done." She grinned. "I think I would like your mother."

"She would like you."

"Does she live close enough to visit?" Rosalyn asked as she followed him down the stairs.

"She's in the Dallas area. I visit as often as I can. Now that I'm out of the military, I hope to make that more often."

"And your father?"

Becker's chest tightened. "He passed away several years ago."

"I'm sorry," she said, her smile slipping. "It's hard to lose someone you love."

He nodded. "Yes, it is. We were all sorry to hear of your loss. We were there when Trace got the news." Becker paused at the bottom of the stairs.

"This way." Rosalyn led him down a hallway, passing the entrance to the kitchen and turning through a doorway into a spacious laundry room with cabinets, countertops and a utility sink. "You can put the basket on the floor. I'll sort the items after breakfast. If you need anything washed, you can leave your things in the laundry room. We'll get around to it today."

"Thank you. I'm all caught up."

They walked into the kitchen in companionable silence.

Trace was pouring water into the repository of the coffee maker. "I hope you like your coffee strong," he called out over his shoulder. "We need it after last night."

Matt entered the kitchen, his hair damp, wearing a T-shirt and faded blue jeans. His feet were bare, and dark shadows lingered beneath his eyes. He stopped in the middle of the kitchen and stretched his arms above his head, working the kinks out of his body.

"Long night?" Rosalyn asked. "Did you sleep at all?"

Matt dropped his arms to his sides. "No, ma'am," he said. His gaze met Becker's. "But we have most of the information you'll need to infiltrate the black market–art circles. Apparently, there's an entire group of dirty-rich patrons of the arts who are willing to spend big bucks on hot commodities."

"Great."

Trace pulled coffee mugs out of the cabinet and lined them up on the counter in front of the coffee maker. "We found your guy."

"Really?" Becker crossed his arms over his chest, his interest piqued. "Who will I be impersonating?"

"Gunter Kraus," Trace said.

Matt stepped in. "He's a little older than you, at forty-two, but approximately the same height and coloring, with blond hair and blue eyes." He pulled out his cell phone and brought up an image of the man in question wearing a black tuxedo with a red rose pinned to the lapel. On his arm was a beautiful woman with raven-black hair and dark eyes. She wore a striking red dress, the front of which plunged all the way down to her belly button.

Becker tipped his head toward the cell phone. "Who's the woman?"

"Monique Jameson," Matt answered. "We found her in a number of the photographs. She appears to be one of his regulars."

"Good. Her coloring is similar to Olivia's."

"We thought so too," Trace said.

Becker took the phone and studied the man. "Do we have any videos on this guy?"

Matt nodded. "After breakfast, I'll show you what we found. This guy is internationally known as a playboy. He gets what he likes because he has a massive trust fund and investments he inherited from his father and grandfather. From what we learned from the dark web, he likes to collect artwork to display in his château in the Swiss Alps."

Trace added, "He isn't too concerned about following laws. He thinks his wealth makes him exempt from rules others have to follow. He was a suspect in the disappearance of a young college girl on vacation at a resort in Mexico. The case was swept under the rug before it could make it to the Mexican court."

"Did they ever find the girl?"

"No." Trace's lips pressed together in a tight line.

Matt crossed the kitchen to stand beside Trace at the coffee maker. "Gunter arrived on a Greek island two days ago. His reservation at a resort there indicates he'll be there a week."

Becker nodded. "So we can be relatively assured he isn't coming to America anytime soon."

Matt shook his head. "You'll have to be flexible. The man has a fleet of jets at his disposal and he's been known to change his mind. He could be back in the States as we speak or within a few hours. The only reason we don't think he's here now is because he likes to be the center of attention."

Trace nodded. "Where he goes, the paparazzi follow. We'd know if he was stateside." He picked up the carafe of coffee, poured a mug full and held it out to Matt. "Coffee?"

"Yes." Matt took the mug and sipped the steaming brew. He closed his eyes and sighed. "Man, I needed that."

Trace poured another cup and offered it to Becker. "Think you can pull off impersonating this guy?"

Becker took the mug, breathing in the fragrant aroma mixed with the steam. He dared to sip the liquid before answering, "My German is rusty."

"No worries. He was raised in the US in a posh penthouse apartment in New York City." Trace poured another cup of coffee and handed it to his mother. "I doubt he learned to speak much German, despite his heritage."

Still holding Matt's phone with the picture of Gunter, Becker nodded. "In that case, I can do it."

"Then we'll need to make sure you're equipped with everything you'll need to be convincing."

"Like…?" Becker cocked an eyebrow. He had an idea of what he'd need, but he wanted to hear what Trace and Matt considered important.

"Clothes," Rosalyn piped in. "If Gunter is a playboy, he probably dresses to the nines in the latest men's fashions, showing off his wealth."

"He likes Ferraris," Matt said.

Trace leaned against the counter and sipped his own coffee. "I have a friend who owns a black Ferrari Enzo."

Matt straightened, his eyes widening. "An Enzo?"

Trace nodded. "A 2003."

Matt let loose a long, low whistle. "Did you know they have 650 ponies and can go 0 to 60 in 3.1 flat?"

Trace nodded.

"Does he owe you a favor?" Becker asked.

Trace's lips quirked at the corners. "He does."

"Must be a big one, if you think he'll loan you his Enzo," Matt said. "I wouldn't let that car out of my sight, much less loan it to a stranger."

"He will. He has a whole collection of expensive sports cars and planes."

"Who did you kill for him?" Matt asked.

Trace's brow wrinkled. "*Kill?* No. It's nothing like that."

"He'll do it for me," Rosalyn interjected. "Ross has always had a…thing for me. When James was murdered, he offered to help. He said if there was anything I needed—anything—he was there for us."

"Does rescuing a kidnapped stranger qualify as anything?" Olivia asked from the entrance to the kitchen.

Becker turned toward the woman who was quickly capturing his heart. She was wearing the clothes Rosalyn had provided the night before. She'd brushed her hair back from her forehead and secured it in a ponytail at the base of her neck, making her look younger and more vulnerable.

The older woman nodded. "If it's important to me, he'll live up to his promise." She crossed the room to take Olivia's hands in hers. "It's important to me for us to find your sister."

Olivia's eyes filled. "Thank you."

Rosalyn gave her a quick hug and then marched to the refrigerator. "I'll have breakfast ready in less than fifteen minutes. Trace, pop some bread in the toaster. Matt, slap some bacon on the griddle."

"I'll set the table." Lily entered the kitchen and went straight for the cabinet with the plates.

"I'll help." Olivia took the stack of plates while Lily grabbed glasses from another cabinet.

A pretty woman with red hair and green eyes staggered into the melee, yawning. "What can I do?"

"Sit and drink some coffee," Rosalyn said. "Matt?"

"On it." Matt paused in his effort to stretch strips of bacon on the griddle. He hurried over to the coffee maker, poured a cup and carried it to the table.

Becker took over at the griddle, finishing what Matt had started. He manned the bacon, careful to let the slices cook to a perfect crispness without burning.

Working together, they had breakfast on the table in the fifteen minutes Rosalyn had promised.

Irish arrived at the back door as Rosalyn was setting the platter of scrambled eggs in the middle of the large kitchen table. He grinned and clapped his hands together. "Did I time that right or what?"

"Perfect," Rosalyn said. "Where's Tessa?" She turned to add another plate and silverware to the table.

"She had to work at the hospital today," Irish said. He claimed a seat at the table. "I stopped by the sheriff's office. Levi and Dallas are following up on a report out of Fort Worth about an abandoned black SUV with damage to the front of the vehicle."

Olivia sank into a seat on the opposite side of the table. "Do they know who it belonged to?"

Irish nodded, took a slice of toast off the top of the stack and laid it on his plate. "It had been reported as stolen yesterday morning from a limousine service in Dallas."

Becker took a seat beside Olivia, noting how her shoulders sagged at the news. "At least we know she's probably somewhere in the Dallas/Fort Worth area."

She shot a glance in his direction. "There are over seven million people in that area. How will we find just one? And they aren't going to make it easy."

"We'll find her," Becker promised. He wasn't sure how, but he'd do everything in his power to make it happen.

"So what's the latest?" Irish asked as he

scooped eggs onto his plate and piled several slices of bacon on top.

Matt filled him in on what they'd learned about Gunter Kraus.

Irish grinned. "Gunter, huh?" His eyes narrowed. "I can see it. The blond hair and blue eyes…"

"The real Gunter Kraus is blond-haired and blue-eyed," Trace said. "And he's in Europe."

"Even better. If you're impersonating someone, it's good if he doesn't show up where you're pretending to be him." Irish laughed. "That would be awkward."

"And potentially deadly," Becker added, his gaze going to Olivia.

She lifted her chin. "I don't care how dangerous. I'm going with you. I've seen some of the news articles on Kraus. He's a player, and he always has a woman on his arm. You show up without one, and they might get suspicious."

"Good point," Trace said. "But maybe we should recruit Dallas, instead of sending you. She's a trained law enforcement officer and was in the army. She might be better suited for the undercover work."

Olivia's gaze went from Trace to Becker. "She's my sister. If you don't take me, I'll find a way in by myself. I won't be left behind."

And Becker wouldn't be able to pull off his

part knowing Olivia was somewhere else, possibly getting into trouble. "You're going with me," he said. "But I expect you to do what I say. Both of our lives could depend on it."

She nodded, her jaw set. "I might not be combat trained, but I will have your back. And I was a pretty good actor in my theater class in high school." Olivia gave him a crooked smile. "I promise not to do anything stupid."

Becker wasn't so concerned about her doing something stupid as he was about the mafia getting wind of their deception and taking matters into their own hands. Whether the Romanos or the Salvatores were responsible for the attack on Olivia's home, one thing was certain: they weren't averse to playing rough.

OLIVIA PUSHED THE FOOD around on her plate. She couldn't focus on eating when she was faced with the prospect of walking into the belly of a mafia family, pretending to be someone she wasn't. If she slipped up and exposed them, they could both end up at the bottom of a lake, wearing concrete shoes. Then Jasmine would be on her own.

She squared her shoulders and forced the dark thoughts from her mind. Their undercover operation would work. It had to.

"Excuse me." Trace laid down his fork and

pushed back from the table. "I need to make a few phone calls." He left the room, and the conversation turned to everyday life on the ranch. Lily and Rosalyn discussed the chores that needed to be completed since the ranch foreman had left before sunup to secure Olivia's house.

Irish and Matt offered to take care of feeding the livestock. When the meal concluded, they all pitched in to clean up.

After the last dish was dried and stored in the cabinet, Lily glanced at Olivia. "Let's get you ready to go shopping."

"'Shopping'?" Olivia frowned. "I don't need to go shopping, but I would like to go back to my house to get some of my belongings."

"You won't have time." Trace entered the room. "You and Beck need to be at the airport in fifteen minutes."

Olivia's heart skipped several beats. "What? Why?"

Trace grinned. "Like Lily said, you're going shopping."

"Why do we need to go to the airport to do that?" Olivia asked.

"Because Whiskey Gulch doesn't have what you and Beck will need to pull off this charade." He tipped his head toward Becker. "I've arranged for you two to fly to San Antonio, where you will be met with a car and taken to the upscale

La Cantera shops. There, you'll be outfitted with clothes befitting a wealthy jet-setter."

"Shouldn't we do that in Dallas?" Olivia protested. "We'd be closer to where we need to be."

Trace shook his head. "With Kraus, it's all about being the center of attention. I'm working on your entrance. You need to be in full Kraus form when you land in Dallas."

"In the meantime, you need something nice to wear when you arrive in San Antonio," Lily said, ushering her out of the kitchen. "I have a dress that might do, even if you're a few inches taller than me." She glanced down at her feet. "And I think we might be close to the same shoe size."

"Just so you know," Olivia said, "I can pay for my own clothes. I might be homeless, but I'm not broke."

"Sure, honey," Lily said. "But I'm betting you don't have an outfit that Gunter Kraus would appreciate."

"And you do?"

"Sweetie, I have some connections of my own." Lily led her up the stairs to the room she shared with Trace.

Olivia had lived in Whiskey Gulch all her life, so she knew what Lily's mother had done to provide for her daughter. The woman had used the only skills she possessed to put food on the table and clothes on Lily's back.

Lily had paid the price for her mother's profession. Many of the boys in school had thought she was as loose as her mother and had hit on her every chance they got. Her father—a liar, thief and swindler—had been a piece of work as well.

Olivia admired Lily for emerging from her crummy childhood a strong, independent woman who could stand up for herself.

Lily flung open her closet door and dug into the back behind hangers holding jeans, chambray shirts and sundresses. After a few swear words, she pulled out a sleeveless off-white dress with simple lines and a narrow black belt.

She held it up. "It was my mother's, a gift from a gentleman…friend. I tossed most of her clothes, but this one was too nice to burn."

Olivia held up her hands. "I can't wear that. It would fit you perfectly, but you're a lot shorter. That dress would be a miniskirt on me."

Lily grinned. "I know, right? It will be perfect for a woman Gunter Kraus would be with. I saw the photos of the women he surrounds himself with. All I can say is that they show a lot of skin."

Olivia stared at the pretty dress with the

plunging neckline and short skirt. "I don't know. It's not me."

"And you won't be you when you're with Gunter Kraus. It's all part of the act." She shoved the dress into Olivia's arms, turned her toward the adjoining bathroom and gave her a gentle shove. "Try it on. It will at least get you to the stores, where you can buy designer outfits. Just remember—when you do purchase clothes, they have to fit the lifestyle you want to portray."

Lily was right. Olivia had never been a risk-taker where her own clothing was concerned. Since she worked with wet clay, she preferred to wear jeans and a heavy apron. Anything else would be ruined. Whenever she dressed up, it was usually in light cotton sundresses or tailored trousers and modest tops.

She entered the bathroom and jumped when the door clicked shut behind her.

"I can do this," she whispered to herself.

"Yes, you can," Lily said through the wood panel.

Olivia grinned. "You weren't supposed to hear that."

"You're going to be fine. Just remember who you're supposed to be."

Olivia shed the clothes she had on. The neckline of the dress was so low, she couldn't wear a bra with it. She slipped out of the undergarment as well and pulled the dress over her head.

It slid over her curves, the material lying soft against her skin. The hem stopped just below the slope of her buttocks.

Olivia faced herself in the mirror and gasped.

"Does it fit?" Lily asked. "Can I come in?"

"Yes, sort of. And yes," Olivia responded, staring at the alluring woman in the mirror. Never in her life had she considered herself sexy. But in that dress...

The door burst open, and Lily swept in, coming to an abrupt halt as her gaze landed on Olivia. Her eyes grew wide, and her mouth dropped open. "Wow." She shook her head and repeated, "Wow."

Heat rose up Olivia's neck and covered her cheeks. She chewed on her lip as she continued to stare at her reflection. "It's too much, isn't it?"

"Not at all," Lily said. "It's perfect for a little shopping spree in the Alamo City. Come on—you don't want to waste time. Trace has a tight schedule he's working with."

"Right." Olivia followed Lily into the bedroom. "I really feel like shopping will waste even more time."

"I know. You want to get to your sister. But you won't fool anyone if you don't dress the part." Lily dived back into the closet, coming up with a pair of black stiletto slides to match the belt. "These might be a little small, but they should work."

Olivia slid her feet into the shoes and tried walking in them. "I'm likely to kill myself in these."

"Practice. You need to be convincing." Lily turned toward the door. "Come on. Trace is waiting in the truck."

Olivia held on to the rail as she descended the stairs and walked out onto the porch.

Irish was standing beside a black pickup while Trace sat behind the steering wheel. "Wow," Irish said under his breath when he caught sight of Olivia.

Becker rounded the front of the truck and held out his hand to her.

She laid her palm in his.

"You look amazing," he whispered, his gaze seeming to drink her in.

Warmth rushed through her body, reminding her of the night they'd spent together. How she wished they could turn back the clock and crawl into bed and forget about impersonating playboys and deceiving the mafia. "Thank you."

"Ready?"

No.

But she nodded and let him help her up into the front passenger seat.

All the while, she tugged at the hem, certain she was exposing more of herself than she intended as she climbed up on the running board and settled on the leather seat.

Becker and Irish settled into the back seat as Trace hightailed it off the ranch.

THE LITTLE AIRPORT outside of Whiskey Gulch wasn't much more than a landing strip for private planes and crop dusters.

Olivia had driven past it all her life, every time she headed to Austin or San Antonio, and never gave it much thought.

Trace drove right up to the runway, where a plane was taxiing to a stop.

The pilot cut the engine, and the propeller slowed to a stop.

A hatch opened on the side of the aircraft before a set of stairs was lowered to the ground. A man poked his head out. "Trace, I got here as soon as I could."

Trace hopped out of his truck and crossed the tarmac to shake the pilot's hand. "Good to see you, Pete. Thanks for coming on short notice."

"Glad to do it," Pete said. "I needed to get some flight time in to keep current on my license. This gives me a good excuse to get the plane out of the hangar."

Pete ducked back into the plane to allow the others to climb aboard and settle in the leather seats.

Trace made quick introductions.

Pete gave them a brief description of the safety features on the aircraft as he secured the door and slipped into the pilot's seat, settled his headset over his ears and started the engine.

Trace sat in as copilot. Pete handed him a headset and went through his checklist before he turned the plane around and took off down the runway.

Olivia had never flown in a plane this small. She wasn't sure she was going to like it.

As the aircraft left the ground, she gripped Becker's hand.

Once they reached their cruising altitude high above the rugged terrain of the Texas Hill Country, Olivia willed herself to relax and take in the scenery below.

Without a headset, she couldn't hear what Trace and the pilot were saying, nor could she carry on much of a conversation with Becker or Irish.

She sat back and thought about what was ahead when they reached Dallas. Shopping in San Antonio would give her a chance to practice her role in front of people. She and Becker had to be convincing if they hoped to fit in and find her sister.

Oh, Jasmine.

Olivia's stomach knotted whenever she thought about her. She'd been so scared. She prayed she was okay and that the men who'd stolen her away hadn't hurt her. If Trace and Becker had theorized correctly and the Romanos had been the ones to kidnap Jasmine, they would want to keep her alive until the Salvatores handed over the painting.

She clung to their assumption, unwilling to imagine the alternative.

Chapter Seven

The trip to San Antonio usually took a couple of hours by car. Flying cut that time in half. They landed at a small airport to the northwest of the city, where a black Suburban waited for them in the parking lot.

They thanked Pete and crossed the tarmac to climb into the SUV. The driver took them along Interstate 10 to La Cantera, a posh shopping center located on the outskirts of the city.

"We have exactly one hour to get what we need and meet back here," Trace informed them as the driver pulled into the parking lot.

"One hour?" Olivia shook her head. "I don't even know where to start."

Trace climbed out of the vehicle and held the door open for Olivia. "My mother called ahead. She has a fashion consultant standing by to help. All we have to do is deliver you to the shop, and the consultant will take over."

Seeming relieved, Olivia sighed. "Thank goodness. I'm clueless when it comes to style."

"You'd look good in anything," Becker assured her. "I think that dress you're wearing now is amazing."

Trace nodded, leading the way. "It is, but you'll need more than one outfit—and the bigger the designer name, the better. The shop also has a makeup artist. They'll do it today and, if need be, show you how to apply it yourself."

"This is insane," Olivia said. "All that can't be done in an hour."

"It can," Trace said. "Let the professionals handle it."

The shopping center was an outdoor mall, tastefully designed and landscaped to encourage shoppers to take their time and spend their entire day visiting the array of stores.

Trace led her straight to one of the high-end women's shops and paused outside the door. "This is your stop. We'll be back to get you when we're done."

Becker didn't like leaving Olivia alone. He would be with his team; she had no one.

A well-dressed woman stepped through the entrance, her gaze sweeping Olivia from top to bottom. "Are you Miss Swann?"

Olivia nodded. "I am."

"Please, come right in so we can get started.

We understand you only have a limited amount of time. Mrs. Travis called ahead with your size requirements and style preferences. We have items ready for your approval, and our makeup artist standing by."

Becker grinned as the woman took charge and whisked Olivia through the door.

If he'd been skeptical about adhering to the hour, he wasn't anymore.

"Come on, Beck," Trace said. "She's in good hands."

Becker had always known that Trace came from money. But it was never more apparent than at that moment. The man was as comfortable in jeans and riding a horse as he was in an expensive men's store, selecting button-down shirts and tailored trousers suitable for someone like Gunter Kraus, who had more money than sense.

Becker had never owned an outfit that cost more than what he could afford with his army paycheck. The fabric quality was amazing and felt good against his skin, but the cost left him feeling uncomfortable.

"Don't think about it," Trace said, as if reading his mind. "Consider it your uniform for the job. The company will cover the expense. Besides, you're now Gunter Kraus. He wouldn't give it a second thought."

With his role in mind, Becker lifted his chin and practiced the entitled sneer he'd noticed on Gunter Kraus's face in all his photographs.

For a man with as much money as Gunter had, he didn't appear terribly happy in any of his pictures.

"There! That's what I'm talking about." Trace grinned. "You have his look."

Becker didn't need the fancy clothes, expensive sport cars or castles in Switzerland to be happy. All he needed was a modest roof over his head, good friends, and a woman who appreciated him and the simpler things in a life.

As he selected a suit, a couple of shirts, casual trousers and a leather jacket, he wondered how Olivia was getting along with her team.

Based on how overwhelmed she'd appeared, she was probably a lot like him. Then again, she'd rocked that dress Lily had loaned her. He couldn't wait to get back to Olivia.

Forty-five minutes into their shopping trip, Becker had what he needed, including underwear, socks and matching shoes. Trace and Irish bought black trousers, black shirts, ties and black suit jackets to look the part of Gunter's usual bodyguard entourage. They dressed in their new clothes and bagged their jeans and T-shirts.

Trace had purchased suitcases and a garment bag from another store while Becker had worked with the salesman. As Becker and the sales team selected items, Trace had a clerk ring them up, remove the tags, steam any wrinkles out and add them to the garment bag or suitcase.

Becker tried to draw the line when Trace insisted on purchasing a Rolex watch. Trace won the argument, and the watch was added to the stack.

By the time they left the store, they'd racked up thousands of dollars in purchases.

"Wow," Becker said, still in sticker shock. "That was a lot of money."

"Look, I don't expect you to pay for all of this," Trace said. "I just don't want you walking into a hostile environment without the tools you need to convince them not to kill you." He gave Becker a brief grin. "You're part of the team. My friend and brother. I want this plan to work."

"It *will* work," Becker said. It had to. Not only did he have to find Jasmine, but he also had to prove to Trace he hadn't made a mistake in hiring him.

Leaving the army had been one of the hardest things Becker had ever done. It had meant leaving the family of brothers he'd been with through some of the hardest times he'd ever endured.

Having a job to go to with some of his brothers in arms had been his saving grace—a job working with the men he'd fought alongside and trusted with his life. It had been a godsend. He owed Trace more than money could ever buy. The man had thrown him a lifeline into the civilian world when he'd left everything he'd known.

Two minutes after they left the men's shop, they arrived in front of the store where they'd left Olivia.

Before Becker could reach for the handle, the door opened, and a woman stepped out.

For a split second, he didn't recognize her—but only for a split second. She wore a bloodred dress in a silky, flowing material that hugged every inch of her delectable body, from the fullness of her breasts to the narrowing curve of her waist and the gentle swell of her hips. The hem stopped a few inches short of midthigh, exposing her incredibly long and beautiful legs, trim ankles and sparkling rhinestone-encrusted high heels.

Her black hair had been swept back from her forehead and hung straight down, with a delicate loose curl caressing her cheek.

The subtle colors of the makeup enhanced the natural beauty of her skin, while bold eye shadow illuminated her eyes.

She was drop-dead gorgeous—nothing like

the woman with mud up to her elbows and smudges on her face who'd captured his heart.

She walked toward him.

No…she *stalked* him like a cat on the prowl.

When she stopped in front of him, his pulse kicked into high gear.

"Hey, good-looking," she said in a low, sultry tone that set his blood on fire. She leaned into him and trailed her finger along the hard line of his jaw. "Let's say you and I blow this joint and head for Big D."

His hands automatically rose to encircle her waist. He had to swallow, hard, to get his tongue to move. "If by Big D, you mean Dallas, I'm game, sweetcakes. Lead the way."

Irish laughed out loud. "Dude, you should see your face. Priceless."

Olivia frowned. "Did I get it right? I was channeling my inner vamp. I practiced that line in my head a hundred times. Was it not at all convincing?"

Irish snorted. "Not convincing? Beck's tongue practically hit the floor. He knows you, and he was completely convinced."

Trace shook his head. "You need to work on your inner sleaze, man. Kraus would have been all over her in a heartbeat. He's not known for being subtle or a gentleman."

"I'll get it right. I just wasn't expecting…

this." His gaze swept Olivia from head to toe. Everything about her was perfect: the clothes, the hair and the makeup.

Becker was attracted to her in a big way. But he more so wanted the woman who'd lain naked with him last night. Her hair had been mussed, and she hadn't worn fancy clothes or expensive shoes, but she'd made love with him without holding back. She was passionate and sexy without even trying.

He tightened his hold around her waist. "Hey, doll," he said. "Want to have dinner with me tonight in Paris?"

She shook her head and walked her fingers across his chest. "That would take too long."

"How about I fly you to the moon and back?"

Her lips curled. "Now you're talking."

"Give me a little time, and I'll do just that." He turned her toward the parking lot. "In the meantime, life's one big adventure if you stick with me."

"I'm counting on it," she said and crossed one leg in front of the other, walking with a pronounced swing to her hips.

Becker liked how Olivia had thrown herself into the role of Monique Jameson. Now, if he could quit drooling over her and get himself together, they might just pull it off.

OLIVIA WALKED BESIDE BECKER, loving the feeling of his arm around her, holding her close against him. She'd even liked coming on to him as if she were the real Monique Jameson and he was Gunter Kraus. The surprise in his eyes had quickly changed to heat.

The dress had done its job. If Becker had been that distracted, surely the mafia members—being mostly virile males—would find it difficult to focus on hurting her or Becker. And while she held their attention, Becker, Trace and Irish could look for clues that would lead them to Jasmine.

The SUV hadn't moved from where the driver had parked. As soon as they were all on board, the driver shifted into gear and pulled out of the parking lot and out onto the highway leading into San Antonio.

"Aren't we flying out of the same airport we flew into?" Olivia asked.

Trace shook his head. "The runway is a little short for the jet to land on."

Olivia sat back against the leather upholstery and cocked an eyebrow at Trace's back. "We didn't fly in a jet. I distinctly recall a prop on that plane."

Trace shot a glance over his shoulder. "We're not flying out in the plane we flew in on."

Olivia's brows rose. "No?"

"No," Trace said. "We're flying to Dallas in a jet."

"A jet." Olivia's brow dipped. "Wouldn't it just be faster to drive? It takes almost as much time to clear security checkpoints."

Trace shook his head. "Not at all. We aren't flying commercial. We can be there in minutes versus hours. Let's do this."

The frown on Olivia's face must have tickled Becker's funny bone because he laughed. "What's wrong?" he asked.

Her lips twisted in a wry grin. "My usual day consists of sitting for long hours, shaping pottery in a quiet room all by myself. I'm not sure I'm cut out for the business of espionage."

"Me neither." Becker's brow knit. "But if it's the only choice we have, we'll make it work."

"And we'll be there as backup," Trace said.

During the drive to the airport, Trace was on the phone with Matt, his conversation hushed. Matt must have been doing most of the talking. Olivia wished she could hear what Trace's brother had to say. Hopefully, he had more information that would help them pull this off.

They didn't go to the main terminal where commercial travelers waded through TSA security. Instead, the driver dropped them off at the door to the general aviation entrance.

With his back to the building, Trace addressed the others. "From here on out, you're in character."

Olivia fought the urge to nod. Instead, she flipped her hair back over her shoulder and hooked her arm through Becker's.

Becker raised an eyebrow and stared down his nose at Trace, his friend and boss. "You're in the way."

Trace's lips quirked, but by the time he turned to enter the building, he was all business.

The woman at the counter asked if she could help.

"I'm with Gunter Kraus," Trace said. "Our transport should have arrived by now."

Becker stepped up behind Trace and lifted his nose in the air. "Can we get a move on? I don't want to be late for my massage." He settled a pair of sunglasses on his face and looked toward the sliding glass door leading out onto the tarmac.

The woman behind the counter straightened. "Yes, sir. Your jet arrived five minutes ago. Could I get you a bottle of water to take with you?"

He curled his lip in his best sneer. "A martini would be better."

Her cheeks flushed. "I'm sorry, sir. We don't serve mixed drinks in the FBO."

"That's a pity," Becker said. "If you can't get me a martini, could you at least let us board?

I'm sure my staff will be able to accommodate me."

"Of course." The clerk's cheeks reddened, and she quickly punched a button behind the counter. The glass door slid open. "Have a nice day," she said as Becker strode through with Olivia draped on his arm, followed by Trace and Irish, who looked like bulked-up bodyguards in their solid black ensembles.

A plane about four times larger than the one they'd flown in from Whiskey Gulch stood at the ready. The stairs came down, and a man in black trousers and a white shirt with decorative epaulets stood at attention at the bottom. "Good morning, Mr. Kraus."

Becker sailed past him. "I'll need a dry martini, two olives, before we leave the ground. Monique, be a gem—make sure it's shaken, not stirred."

"Sure, Gunter, baby," Olivia said.

Olivia's low, sexy voice brought images to Becker's mind of her lying naked in bed, writhing beneath him. Now was not the time to get excited. Then again, the element of danger and the secrecy of their undercover operation spiked his adrenaline and desire.

Becker stepped inside the plane and inwardly marveled at the opulence. "Not one of mine," he said, "but it'll have to do."

Trace, Irish and Olivia all sat and pulled their seat belts across their laps.

The male flight attendant who'd greeted them outside the plane leaned close to Becker. "Sir, you'll need to sit and secure your seat belt."

"That martini? Pronto?" He stopped himself short of snapping his fingers, unsure of just how far he should take Gunter's privileged attitude.

The attendant scurried to the other end of the cabin and opened a cabinet, revealing a fully equipped bar.

Becker dropped into the seat beside Olivia and secured his seat belt.

The attendant returned with his drink and hurried to close the door and inform the pilot they were ready to take off.

Minutes later, they were in the air, climbing to altitude above San Antonio, swinging north toward Dallas.

Beside him, Olivia was stiff, her gaze fixed on the window.

Becker reached for her hand and lifted it to brush a kiss across the backs of her knuckles. He too felt the strain of the charade. He sipped on the martini to take the edge off but didn't get too far before he realized he didn't like martinis. In fact, he didn't like gin, preferring beer and whiskey over the fancy drink any day.

He glanced at his watch. Jasmine had been

missing less than twenty-four hours. The sooner they got to Dallas, the sooner they could begin their search for the missing painting, which might be the motive for a murder and the key to finding Olivia's sister.

Becker had been on many dangerous missions during his time as a Delta Force operator. Never had he thought he'd be on one just as dangerous in his own country.

And he was going into the operation unarmed and with an untrained woman at his side. Red flags waved all around him, but it was too late to turn around and come up with a new plan. He and Olivia had to make their way into the inner circles of the black market for illegally acquired works of art. The stakes were high. The people involved wouldn't bat an eye at shooting someone if they thought they would expose them to the authorities.

Becker studied Olivia's profile, regretting his decision to bring her along on this operation. He wasn't sure he could protect himself, but he sure as hell would do his best to protect her.

Chapter Eight

Olivia gripped Becker's hand as the plane landed at one of the small executive airports near Dallas. She never felt comfortable flying.

"Looks like the paparazzi got wind of your arrival, Gunter," Trace commented and winked at Becker. The head of the Outriders had probably let it "leak" that jet-setting playboy Gunter Kraus would be landing in Dallas at that exact airport and approximate time, on a different airplane than one of his own.

A crowd of reporters had gathered on the other side of the fence surrounding the airport.

Trace was on the phone the moment the plane landed and didn't hang up until they'd taxied to the small terminal and come to a full stop.

Becker immediately popped open his seat belt buckle.

Trace pocketed his cell phone and met Becker's gaze. "You have been invited to an exclusive showing at the Madison Gallery in downtown

Dallas at six o'clock this evening. In the meantime, we'll get you and Miss Jameson checked in to your suite at the Ritz-Carlton."

The flight attendant hurried through the cabin to check with the pilot before he hit the switch to lower the stairs. Then he stepped back. "Enjoy your stay in Dallas."

Becker pushed to his feet, held out his hand for Olivia and pulled her up to stand beside him. "You ready?"

"Always, when I'm with you." She ran her hand across his chest and smiled. Pretending to be his girlfriend had its perks. She could touch him as much as she wanted. Monique would be all over Gunter.

Trace was first off the plane, followed by Becker, Olivia and Irish.

Olivia glanced toward the swarm of reporters pressed against the chain-link fence, snapping pictures of Gunter Kraus…or so they thought. Olivia hoped Gunter wasn't one to follow the news on the internet. Their cover would be blown pretty quickly, if he saw someone impersonating him in Dallas, while he was vacationing in Greece.

Becker turned and held out his hand for Olivia as she descended the last step. Then he swung her into his arms and kissed her soundly as cameras clicked and reporters shouted questions about his relationship with Monique. Was she the one? Were wedding bells in the future?

When he set her back on her feet, her heart was pounding, and she felt a little light-headed. Man, he was a good kisser. She could get used to playing Monique to his Gunter.

They passed through the terminal and ran the gauntlet of reporters, with Trace and Irish playing their part as the bodyguards protecting the rich man and his girl.

Several times, a reporter got close enough to shove a microphone in Becker's face.

Becker gave his best sneer for the cameras and moved on without comment, tucking Olivia against his side, shielding her the best he could from the rudest of the paparazzi.

She loved that he was so protective, but she hoped he wouldn't sacrifice his own safety for hers.

A chauffeur in a black suit stood beside a shiny white limousine. As Becker and Olivia approached, he opened the door. Olivia got in first and slid across the seat. Becker dropped in beside her.

The chauffeur closed the door, loaded their luggage and got into the driver's seat. He raised the barrier between the front and back with the push of a button. The window tinting effectively blocked them from the view of the media mongers, giving them a relative sense of privacy.

A black SUV was parked in front of the limousine. The driver got out, handed the keys to Trace and walked away. Trace slipped behind the wheel, Irish took shotgun, and they pulled away from the terminal and out into traffic.

With moderate to heavy traffic flowing through the Dallas metro area, it took thirty minutes to reach the Ritz-Carlton hotel.

Becker spent the time holding Olivia. She assumed he was still playing his part. Having little experience with plush limousines, she didn't know if the driver had access to sound or video of what was going on in the back. Becker and Olivia had to pull off their ruse. They had to get Jasmine back, safe and sound.

The fewer people who knew the truth about Gunter Kraus's visit to Dallas, the better.

Olivia sat beside him, holding his hand like a lifeline. Though she absolutely looked the part of Monique Jameson, she felt as if others would see right through her act. She didn't want to be the one who blew their cover.

When they arrived at the hotel, a bellman was there to collect their luggage from the trunk. The chauffeur got out and opened the door to let them out.

Trace and Irish escorted them into the lobby,

where they were met by the manager, who personally escorted them to the penthouse suite.

Once the manager left and the bellman delivered their suitcases, the room fell silent.

Using a bug detector, Trace and Irish scoured the room, checking beneath table edges, inside lampshades and behind paintings on the wall.

Olivia was amazed at how thorough they were.

Then Trace entered the huge bathroom, turned on the shower faucet and let the water stream down, making enough noise to drown out their words. He waved Becker and Olivia into the bathroom, where they huddled close to hear each other talk.

"You can't be too careful," Trace said. "If people are considering Gunter Kraus as a potential buyer for the stolen painting, they will be watching him closely. That includes bugging your room."

Olivia shivered and wrapped her arms around her middle. The thought of someone spying on them gave her the willies.

"Watch anyone who comes into your room for any reason at all. And perform a bug check every time you leave and come back." Trace looked into their faces, his own tight, concerned. "Keep in mind at all times that whether you're in this room or wandering around Dallas, you will be watched."

Olivia nodded. Dealing with stolen goods would make the buyers and sellers paranoid. And rightly so.

Trace continued. "Once the media releases footage of Gunter arriving in Dallas, word will spread to the two families. That's why we staged that arrival in front of the media. For now, hang tight, relax for a while and then change into evening clothes for the art exhibit. It's by special invitation only. The people who will be there will be wearing their finest."

"What do we hope to achieve at the show?" Becker asked.

"Vincenzo Salvatore is supposed to be there. It's safe to assume he'll be looking for a buyer."

"Like Gunter Kraus," Olivia said.

Trace nodded. "Rumor has it that collectors from all over the world are coming to Dallas or sending representatives in hopes of acquiring the Wyeth painting."

Olivia shivered again. "And all I want is my sister back."

"I read in the news earlier today that Nico will be released tomorrow if they can't produce any substantial evidence that he killed Eduardo. His alibi insists he was with her the entire night. The witness who accused him has gone missing, and they only had her word that she saw him at the gallery that night."

"Won't the Romanos be after him to avenge Eduardo's death?" Olivia asked.

Trace met and held Olivia's gaze. "Not if Nico is the only one who knows where the painting is."

"Thus, the reason for keeping Jasmine alive," Olivia said.

"If Nico is smart, he won't have told anyone where the stolen art is," Becker said. "It's even more reason for his family to want to get him out of jail."

Travis's eyes narrowed. "That painting is going to be worth a lot more on the black market. The Romanos could have lined up a buyer, who might have put down a deposit or actually paid the full price and is waiting for delivery of the product."

"Great motivation to get Nico to reveal the location of the painting," Becker said.

"In exchange for the girl, the Romanos get the Wyeth. Nico gets the witness, and he can do whatever he wants with her to stay out of jail."

Olivia flinched. "There are a lot of moving parts to this story," she noted. "The Romanos can't make their demands until Nico is released and can lead them to the painting."

"They can't kill Jasmine and offer up the

body, because dead people can't testify in court," Becker said. He touched Olivia's arm. "Sorry to be so blunt about your sister—but in this case, it's a good thing that it's more beneficial to them to keep her alive until they have the painting in hand. She's their only leverage."

Olivia's hands curled into fists. "We have to be there if and when an exchange is made."

"Or get to the painting first and make the trade ourselves," Irish said.

"If they release Nico tomorrow—" Trace tipped his head toward Irish "—we'll tail him."

Irish laughed. "You mean *I'll* tail him. Gunter doesn't go anywhere without a bodyguard. And I wouldn't feel right leaving these two without backup."

Trace's mouth twisted. "You're right. Irish would tail Nico." He tapped his chin with the tip of his finger. "I think we could use Matt and Levi up here. I'll step out of the hotel long enough to place a few calls. We can have them in Dallas by morning."

"Matt needs to stay on his hacker and plugged into the internet," Irish said.

"He can do that from here." Trace drew in a deep breath and let it out slowly. "Things might start moving faster if they turn Nico loose. We'll need all the help we can get."

Olivia stood among the men, feeling a little

more hopeful than she had when standing in the middle of her shattered living room, watching the taillights of the stolen SUV disappear along with her sister.

If anyone could pull this operation off, it was the Outriders.

WITH A FEW HOURS to kill before they had to leave for the art exhibit, Becker shrugged out of the casual blazer he wore and stretched out on the bed. He'd learned to rest when he could to conserve energy he might need for later.

Trace and Irish had left the room. Trace would be outside the hotel by now, making arrangements to get Matt and Levi up to Dallas. Irish would be standing outside their door, as the first line of defense for Gunter Kraus.

While Becker lay on the bed, Olivia paced.

"You'll be worn out before we even begin the evening." Becker patted the bed beside him. "Relax."

Olivia snorted. "I can't. I keep thinking of…" She bit her lip to keep from saying the name of her sister. Her heart hurt at the thought of how scared and alone she must be feeling. She was frustrated about doing nothing while her sister suffered.

"You need to have a store of energy in reserve for the night to come." He patted the bed again.

"You won't enjoy the exhibit if you're so tired that you can barely stand."

She slowed to a stop beside the bed. "I know you're right. But it's hard."

"Then fake it until you feel it." He grinned. "That sounded suggestive, didn't it?" He gave her a gentle look. "Do this…" He inhaled and let the air out slowly. "Breathe."

She laughed, but she wasn't smiling. "I can't. I feel like my chest is constricted. I've felt that way since we left this morning."

"Try it with me." He drew in another deep breath.

Olivia pressed a hand to her chest and gave it a shot, pulling in a long breath.

"Now hold it in for a second," he said.

She held it.

"Let it go slowly." His voice was low, rich and resonant.

His words alone slowed her heartbeat. She released the air from her lungs, and her body relaxed a little.

When Becker patted the bed beside him once more, she complied and lay down on the mattress.

The last time she'd been in bed with Becker, they'd been naked—making mad, passionate love.

Now they lay side by side, fully clothed, without touching.

The fact that someone could bug their room at any time made her paranoid. One small mistake had the potential to reveal them as the fakes they were.

Olivia had never been very good at lying. Acting was easier when she memorized the lines; she wasn't as good at ad-libbing. But she'd insisted on being part of the mission to save her sister. She'd better get her act together. Her sister's life and the lives of Becker and his teammates depended on her getting it right.

Becker reached over and took her hand in his, squeezing it gently. "Breathe."

She did, repeating the long, slow inhale-and-release process until it came more naturally. Her muscles relaxed, relieving some of the pressure constricting her chest.

The silence stretched on.

A number of times, she opened her mouth to say something but closed it without uttering a word. She wanted to learn more about this man—who he was, what he wanted out of life, his favorite color, what he liked to eat…everything. All of that discovery would have to wait until they were back in Whiskey Gulch, with her sister safely away from the mafia families using her as a pawn in their tug-of-war over a painting.

Olivia closed her eyes and continued to practice the slow, steady breathing Becker had prescribed.

When she woke, the room was darker; she must have fallen asleep. She reached for Becker, but the bed beside her was empty.

Her pulse quickened, and she sat up straight.

"I'm here," he called out in the huge room.

She turned to find Becker silhouetted against the floor-to-ceiling windows overlooking the Dallas skyline.

"How long was I asleep?" she asked, pushing her hair back away from her face.

"An hour and a half."

"Did I miss anything?"

He chuckled. "Nothing. It's almost time to get ready for the exhibit. I thought we might want to get something to eat along the way."

Her stomach rumbled at the mention of food. "That would be nice." Olivia swung her legs over the side of the bed and stood, smoothing the wrinkles out of her red dress. "Did I hear right? Trace said the patrons of the arts like to dress up for exhibits?"

"That's what he said. What you have on should be fine."

Olivia glanced down at the dress. "I like it, but I have another outfit in mind. The lady at the designer store said a woman can't go wrong with a little black dress. Since the people who attend these events like to dress up, I'll do the same." She gave him a quick smile. "If you want in the bathroom, go now. Once I'm in there, I might not come out until I'm completely ready."

"I'd like to shave before you barricade yourself inside."

She laughed. "Go ahead. I'll gather my clothes and makeup while you're doing your thing."

Becker unearthed a shaving kit from his suitcase and carried it into the bathroom, leaving the door wide open.

Every time Olivia walked past, she couldn't help but look inside.

Becker had removed his shirt and was standing in front of the mirror, rubbing shaving cream across his jaw.

The man was far too attractive for Olivia's own good. It only took her one trip to gather everything she needed; the other trips past the open bathroom door had been out of pure curiosity—and the burning heat that had begun in the pit of her belly and was spreading throughout her body.

She glanced at the clock, wondering if they had enough time to…

With a firm shake of her head, she reminded herself to stick to the plan until they got her sister back. Hopefully, there'd be plenty of time for lovemaking later.

On Olivia's next pass in front of the little bathroom, Becker emerged, his shirt flung over one shoulder, his broad chest naked and sun-kissed.

Olivia's feet slowed as she looked up into his clear blue eyes.

"I'm finished in there," he said. "It's all yours."

She was tempted to run her fingers over his fine chest. They tingled with the memory of doing that the night before. She hoped she'd have another opportunity soon.

For now, she squeezed past him, careful not to touch any of his magnificent flesh. She was already too confused by the desire raging through her to keep her head on straight. One touch might set off a firestorm of desire she wouldn't be able to defuse.

If she gave in, and the man was willing, they'd fall into bed and make love. With Olivia's luck, Trace and Irish would pick that moment to enter the room and catch them in the act.

They could say they were just getting into character, but it would be a lie—and it wouldn't help them free Jasmine either.

She entered the bathroom, closed the door and leaned against the cool wooden panels.

Staying in the same room with Becker could be a joy or a challenge. Olivia struggled to keep her hands off the muscular Delta Force soldier.

Focus.

Olivia changed out of the red dress and into the black one. Her hands shook a little as she reached behind to pull up the zipper.

The art exhibit would be the next big test of their acting skills. Hopefully, they wouldn't run into anyone who knew Gunter or Monique personally. In a world full of people, the rich and famous tended to run in the same circles. That scared Olivia.

Once she had the dress on, she slid her feet into the shiny rhinestone-encrusted shoes she'd purchased at the store and straightened in front of the full-length mirror.

Wow. She looked like a different person from the artist who spent her days with mud up to her elbows. She looked every bit as good as any celebrity in Hollywood or the high rollers in Dallas. Seeing it for herself helped boost her confidence.

They would be in a public place with lots of other people. Hopefully, the Salvatores and the Romanos wouldn't do anything crazy.

Olivia wished she had a weapon she could hide underneath her dress. Not that the dress would hide anything—it fit her body like a second skin, and the slit up the side ran from the floor up to her midthigh. No. Even if she had a knife or small gun, the dress wouldn't hide anything.

If things got crazy, she would have to rely on her charm, wit and her former Delta Force protector.

Chapter Nine

Becker sat in the back seat of the stretch limousine beside Olivia. He'd thought nothing could top that red dress she'd worn earlier. He'd been wrong. The black sheath gracing her lithe body invoked such a rush of desire, he could barely think.

The limousine delivered Becker and Olivia to Madison Gallery, which was not too far from the Ritz-Carlton. A uniformed attendant hurried forward and opened the door.

Reporters stood on either side of the velvet ropes cordoning off the entrance.

As soon as Becker got out, cameras flashed and reporters shouted.

"Mr. Kraus, could you answer a few questions for us?"

"Mr. Kraus, are you and Ms. Jameson engaged? Is there a wedding date set?"

"Gunter, is it true that you fired your former assistant after you got her pregnant?"

Becker ignored the questions and turned to extend his hand to Olivia.

She laid her palm in his and swiveled on the seat. One slender leg emerged through the door, the slit of her dress rising up to the middle of her thigh.

Becker's groin tightened.

Olivia was a beautiful woman. She looked fabulous in that black dress, in the red dress, in jeans and a T-shirt, and in nothing at all. He pulled her to her feet and into his arms. "Do you know just how gorgeous you are?"

She gave him a sultry smile. "You're not so bad yourself."

Then he kissed her in front of the attendants, valets and the army of reporters. He told himself it was what Gunter would do. The truth was, he wanted to kiss her, and he was happy to play the Gunter card to get what he wanted.

She leaned into him, her fingers curling into his shirt, dragging him closer.

For a moment, he forgot where he was, who he was supposed to be and why it was important. It was just him and Olivia.

A honk sounded on the street in front of the gallery, bringing him back to Earth. A black limousine pulled in as their white one drove off.

An attendant opened the door, and a blonde in a long white dress stepped out, her hair swept up and back in a sophisticated style. She smiled and approached them. "Oh, good. I don't have to go in by myself." Her brows rose. "You are going to the exhibit, aren't you?"

Olivia nodded. "We are." She held out her hand. "I'm Monique. This is—"

"Gunter Kraus," the woman said. "I saw the news of your arrival in Dallas on television." She flipped her hair toward the crowd of media personnel snapping photographs. "The paparazzi never leave you alone. How do you put up with it?"

Becker shrugged. "You get used to it." He held out his hand. "And you are?"

"Tacey Rogers, fellow art enthusiast. Do you mind if I go in with you? My date was unavoidably detained. Which is short for, I was stood up."

"Please, join us," Becker said. "The more, the merrier." He held out his elbow to Tacey, as he suspected Gunter would do. Though the man was most often seen with Monique, he was seen with other women as well. Based on the tabloids, he was never one to turn down a pretty woman he might get into his bed later.

Tacey hooked her hand through the crook of his arm and smiled up at him.

Then Becker held out his other elbow to Olivia and winked down at her.

She took his arm, cocking an eyebrow as if questioning his proclivity to collect women.

Gunter wouldn't give it a second thought. He was a ladies' man. The more women who surrounded him, the happier he was.

Becker, on the other hand, was a one-woman man. The kiss he and Olivia shared hadn't been pretense. His only regret was that they weren't alone to enjoy it longer. He hoped to remedy it later when they were back at the Ritz.

"I almost didn't come tonight," Tacey was saying.

"No?" Becker glanced down at the blonde. "Why?"

She grimaced. "Well, after the murder at Cavendish Gallery, I wasn't sure how safe we would be. Frankly, I'm surprised this event wasn't canceled."

"If you were that concerned, why did you come?" Olivia asked.

"Morbid curiosity as to who would show up. I'm betting most of the people coming are more interested in the stolen painting than those on display at this exhibit." She smiled up at Becker. "What about you? Surely you didn't fly all the way into Dallas for this show."

Becker gave a secretive smile. "Let's just say I'm intrigued by the events. Especially considering the Cavendish curator is missing."

Tacey's eyes widened. "She was the one who reported the murder, the only witness who saw Nico Salvatore do it."

Olivia stiffened on Becker's other side.

"Makes you wonder," Becker said, "doesn't it?"

Tacey glanced away. "The Salvatore family want the public to believe the curator did it and got away with the Wyeth painting."

"What do you think?" Becker asked.

"I think Nico did it, and he's the only one who knows where that painting is." Her lips twisted. "If they let him out of jail, you know he'll be followed and he'll be in the market to sell that painting before he gets caught with it. Everything seems to be hinging on a painting no one knew existed until a couple of weeks ago."

"Which makes the event tonight even more interesting," Becker said.

Tacey nodded. "I had to come."

"Why do you think the curator disappeared?" Olivia asked.

The other woman's mouth thinned. "Who knows? If I were her, I'd have kept my mouth shut. Squealing on a Salvatore is like signing your own death certificate."

"Why is that?"

The blonde leaned around Becker, her eyebrows cocked. "Do you really not know?"

Olivia blinked. "Know what?"

Becker almost laughed at her innocent act.

"Nico's father is Vincenzo Salvatore, one of the richest men in the country."

"So?" Olivia quipped.

"*So* he could buy any verdict he wants from any court in the land. He's that rich. And if that didn't work, he could pay to have the accuser silenced."

"Sounds like she put herself in danger," Becker said.

"Yes, she did," Tacey said softly. "I don't think she understood the ramifications. I'll bet she does now."

"You appear to be pretty informed about the art community here in Dallas," Becker said. "Why would Salvatore's son kill a man for a painting if his father could afford to purchase it outright?"

"Eduardo was stupid. He wanted the money the painting would bring on the black market."

"Did he need the money that badly?" Olivia asked.

Tacey snorted. "That's just it—his uncle Giovanni has almost as much money as the Salvatores. Or at least, he did. Who knows, with the world economy the way it is these days? Maybe he lost it in the stock market, or his ships ran aground, or his money manager absconded with it. The Wyeth was estimated to be worth at least three million if sold legitimately."

"Interesting," Becker said.

"Enough to kill for," Tacey said.

By then, they had entered the lobby of the gallery, where other patrons had gathered.

"If the Wyeth is worth so much, it could make sense that the curator might have been in on the whole thing," Becker suggested.

Tacey shook her head. "I think she was in the wrong place at the wrong time and witnessed something she shouldn't have seen. Her biggest mistake was opening her mouth and doing the right thing by reporting a murder. I kind of feel sorry for her, with both families after her."

"*Both* families?" Olivia asked. "I would think the Salvatores would be the only ones wanting her to disappear. Why would the Romanos want her out of the picture?"

Becker was enjoying Olivia's wide-eyed, innocent act.

"Good question," Tacey said. "Why don't you ask them?" She tipped her head toward a man with a shock of white hair, bushy brows and dark eyes. He stood in the middle of a group of bulky-looking men who had to be bodyguards. "That's Giovanni Romano."

The man wasn't paying attention to the people around him. He was glaring at another man across the room.

The other guy was taller, with silvery-gray hair and his head held high, bearing a distinguished presence.

"Who's the silver fox?" Olivia asked.

Tacey laughed. "Giovanni's rival, Vincenzo Salvatore. Both men are from fine Italian stock, with quick Italian tempers. I'm surprised they let them in the gallery at the same time. It's a good thing they have metal detectors at the door."

She looked up at Becker. "Gunter, Monique, thank you so much for accompanying me to the door and helping me save face for having been stood up."

"It was your date's loss and our pleasure."

"Monique." Tacey turned her smile to Olivia. "Thank you for sharing Gunter with me."

"You're welcome."

With those parting words, Tacey left them and walked across the room to join Giovanni Romano.

"If you'll excuse me," Olivia said with a smile, "I'll take a moment in the ladies' room and give Trace a call to have Matt conduct a background check on Ms. Tacey Rogers. She seems to know a lot about the Salvatores and the Romanos."

Becker nodded. "I was about to suggest I do the same."

Olivia shook her head. "You need to stay with the others. You're the potential client in the market for hot paintings. Nobody cares about Monique Jameson or will miss her if she disappears for a few minutes."

"I'll miss you," Becker said, his eyes narrowing. "I don't like you being out of my sight for a moment."

She smiled again and batted her eyelashes at him. "I'll be fine."

Becker's gaze followed Olivia until she disappeared down a corridor. His inclination was to follow her. With both mafia bosses in the room, anything could happen—and he didn't want *anything* to happen to Olivia. He and Trace had discussed wearing listening devices, but they hadn't wanted to risk being caught with them. Cell phones were expected. Being caught with a listening device would send up red flags with the mafia.

Once Olivia was out of sight, he turned his attention to Tacey, who was now talking with Giovanni—and not like casual strangers either. The blonde's brow was creased in a frown, and she appeared to be having harsh words with the man. After a few more moments arguing with him, she left his side.

Giovanni started across the floor, heading for Vincenzo Salvatore.

Becker moved closer, hoping to eavesdrop on any conversation the two rivals might have.

Before the two mafia kingpins could collide, a man with a microphone invited the guests to enter the gallery. A crowd of people surged forward, blocking Giovanni's path to Salvatore.

Salvatore joined the others moving through the double doors into the art gallery. Giovanni altered his trajectory and fell in step with the others, his entourage of bodyguards bringing up the rear.

Becker hung back. He didn't want to enter until he had Olivia in his sights. About the time he was ready to go in search of her, she emerged from the hallway. When she caught sight of him, she nodded, indicating she had completed her mission.

He met her halfway across the floor, slipped an arm around her waist and walked with her into the gallery. He felt better knowing where Olivia was, but he didn't feel good at all about being in the same building as two very powerful men with ties to warring mafia families.

He'd liked it better when he was fighting the Taliban in Afghanistan. At least then he had been armed and could defend himself and his team. Here, in what most people considered a more civilized environment, he didn't know who might be the enemy or what he would do if someone decided to raid the party and shoot everyone in the room.

ALTHOUGH OLIVIA GLANCED briefly at the works displayed, she spent more time studying the people around them. If this was truly where they intended to make the exchange, the folks milling around were willing to take risks and break the rules to get what they wanted.

The patrons wandered from room to room, admiring the artwork of a number of artists, local and nationwide. Different rooms had different themes: one was impressionist; another, realist; and yet another contained art employing odd textures and different mediums.

When Olivia stepped into the farthest room, she immediately understood why the exhibit within was so much more special than the others. Each painting on the wall was on loan from the estate of Andrew Wyeth. Several of the patrons were gathered in this room, admiring some of Wyeth's most famous works.

Security guards stood inside the room to ensure no one got close enough to damage or steal anything.

Everyone, including Becker and Olivia, stared

at the displays, enchanted by the realism of each of his works. The man truly had been talented.

"Now can you see why someone would want one of his paintings?" a feminine voice whispered into Olivia's ear.

Tacey stood to her right, her gaze on a portrait of a woman in a field. "This one, like so many others, makes you feel. If it doesn't, it makes you wonder what the woman in the field is feeling. You can practically smell the grass." Tacey inhaled and let the air out slowly. "I know who you are."

Olivia froze, her eyes still on the woman in the painting, not the one who could rat her out to anyone who might take issue with her stolen identity. She was only slightly relieved by the unarmed security officers in the room.

"I don't know what you mean," Olivia said.

"You're not Monique Jameson."

"Yes, I am," Olivia argued in as calm a voice as she could while her heart pounded in her chest. She was terrified their op had been compromised before they had located the painting or Jasmine.

Tacey shot a quick glance her way. "I wish I could say I don't care who you are—but, as it happens, I do care. And that's what will end up getting us both in trouble."

Olivia shook her head. "I don't understand."

"You will. Now, shut up and listen. We don't have much time before others get suspicious. And don't look at me." Tacey tipped her head as if trying to get a different perspective of the painting on the wall. "Monique and Gunter are still island-hopping in Greece."

Olivia drew in a deep breath, ready to refute Tacey's claim.

Tacey continued before Olivia could say anything. "I spoke with Monique this morning and asked her how Gunter was doing. You see, Monique and I met the last time she and Gunter were in Dallas for an art show. We bonded over the fact that neither one of us cared much for expensive art. She'd never tell Gunter that. He's obsessed with owning something that other people could never have. When you're that wealthy, and can have anything you want, finding something unique becomes a challenge. They were on a yacht in Mykonos, about to head for Santorini. Don't worry. I think I'm the only one here who knows this. But that's not the point. When I told you I felt sorry that the curator disappeared, I meant it."

Olivia's heart beat faster. She pressed a hand to her chest, sure everyone near her could hear it.

"Just so you know," Tacey whispered, "she's still alive."

Relief washed through Olivia.

"I've seen her," Tacey said. "Spoken to her. Sat in the same room with her."

Olivia fought the urge to look toward Tacey.

"I wasn't sure at first, but now I know—" Tacey paused and pointed at the painting on the wall as if commenting on some aspect of the work "—you're her sister, Olivia."

"How—"

"She described you as having beautiful black hair and green eyes." Tacey's lips turned up at the corners. "Monique has black hair and gray eyes. She's a little taller than you and maybe a little thinner. She was a model before she hooked up with Gunter. Most people wouldn't pick up on the differences between you and her."

Olivia didn't care at all about Monique, how tall she was, or if she slept on the right side of the bed or the left. All she wanted to know was how to find Jasmine. "Where is she?" she said in a low whisper.

"In one of Romano's warehouses, the last time I saw her," Tacey said.

"Why are they keeping her?"

Tacey gave her another wry smile. "I would think it's obvious. They want the painting, like every other collector in this room. The curator is in a warehouse near the south Dallas train yard. I saw her last night, but there's no guarantee she's still there."

"Why are you telling me this if you're on *their* side?"

"I don't believe in trading a life for a painting." She shrugged. "I told you, I'm not a big fan of art. Not like some who would kill to own that Wyeth original."

"The address?"

"I want to go there first and let you know if she's still there."

"Let me go with you," Olivia begged.

"Can't. Not only would that reveal the fact I told you, but it would also be a waste of time if they've already moved her."

"I'm willing to take the risk."

"I'm not. I'll text you the location once I've made sure she's there."

"You'll need my number."

"Tell me what it is," Tacey said. "I have a good memory."

Olivia told her the number.

Tacey repeated it verbatim.

"How is she?" Olivia asked.

"Shh," Tacey said. "Someone's headed our way."

A stately older man in a black tuxedo with a balding head stopped behind them and studied the painting of the woman.

As one, Olivia and Tacey moved to another work—a watercolor of a seascape in various tones of blues and greens. Keeping her tone low, Tacey leaned slightly toward Olivia. "Hang tough until I send you the location."

Olivia nodded. "Thank you."

"Don't thank me until you get her away from Giovanni and his family."

"Why are you doing this?" Olivia asked. "Won't you be in trouble with the Romanos?"

"I already am. I'm tired of all the drama and corruption. I don't agree with using an innocent as leverage. And they don't really care about their own. They sent Eduardo—the only good man of the lot—to steal the painting as a test of his loyalty to the family." Her chin lifted, and the lines around her mouth deepened. "They were more upset about losing the painting than losing a family member."

Olivia's heart constricted. This woman was putting her life on the line to save a stranger. "Will you be okay?"

"One way or another." She turned away from the painting and smiled at a woman across the room. "Mrs. Mortenson," she called out, "I haven't seen you in forever. How is your son, the doctor?" Tacey left Olivia standing in front of the seascape.

For a long moment, Olivia continued to face

the painting on the wall without seeing it. Her head spun and her heart raced. They'd come to the exhibit to learn where the missing Wyeth was. But now…

An arm slipped around her and pulled her against a solid wall of muscle.

Becker.

Olivia leaned into him, absorbing his strength.

"She knows," she whispered softly.

Chapter Ten

Becker had been across the room, pretending to admire a landscape while doing his best to eavesdrop on a heated conversation between Salvatore and Romano. The two men spoke in hushed tones, and Becker hadn't been able to hear enough to make sense of their words. When he moved closer, they moved away to continue their discussion.

He'd seen Tacey approach Olivia. At first, he thought they were just discussing the artwork in front of them. But when Olivia stiffened, Becker knew it was more important than opinions on style and color. He'd given them the space to finish their conversation. When Tacey moved off to speak with another guest, Becker went to Olivia.

She was holding it together like a champ, but he could tell by the tightness around her mouth and the way she curled her fingers into fists that her control was slipping.

"She knows about us?" Becker asked.

Olivia nodded and looked up at him. "And where they're keeping her."

He forced a smile as he looked down into her eyes. They had to appear to be the carefree playboy and his girlfriend, even when they were on the verge of getting the information they were after. "Where?"

"She said she would text the location when she was certain they hadn't moved her. She did say she was being held in a warehouse on the south side of Dallas, near the train yard."

Becker's brow furrowed. He wasn't sure he trusted the woman. "Why would she tell you that?"

Olivia shook her head. "I think she was in love with Eduardo."

"The victim?"

"If not in love, she cared about him, and his death made her realize the Romano family isn't where she wants to be." Olivia glanced toward the door. "Look."

The woman in question was leaving the Wyeth room.

"Does that mean you're ready to go?"

"Have you accomplished what you came here to do?" She looked around at the other men and women in the room. "Have you sufficiently networked to ensure an invite to any potential sale?"

Becker shook his head. "I have yet to gain an audience with either Salvatore or Romano."

She gave him a tight smile. "Then we need to make that happen before we leave." Her gaze swept the room again, and she paused.

Following her glance, Becker saw that Salvatore was finally alone, studying the painting Tacey and Olivia had been standing in front of.

"There's a painting you need to see." Olivia hooked his elbow and marched him over to where Salvatore stood.

"I think this is my favorite so far," Olivia said as they approached the silver-haired man. "What do you think?"

Salvatore nodded. "It has merit. I appreciate the realism in the artist's work."

"It makes me wonder about the painting that disappeared from Cavendish Gallery. I would like to have observed it in person to see if it elicits the same emotion. What do you think? Did it make you feel the same?"

"I would like to say it does, but I have not had the pleasure of viewing it, other than the image presented in the media. I was unable to make it to Cavendish before its untimely disappearance." His lip curled into a snarl. "Did you come over to accuse my son of murder and stealing the Wyeth too?"

Olivia's eyes widened. "Of course not, Mr. Salvatore. It's just that Gunter and I are big fans of Andrew Wyeth's creations. We wish we'd been able to see that painting before it disappeared."

"You and many others," Salvatore said, his tone abrupt. His glance moved to Becker. "I understand you have quite the collection of artwork in your château in Switzerland."

"I do," Becker said. "It's an expansive château, with room for more."

Salvatore's eyes narrowed and shifted from Olivia to Becker. His gaze held Becker's for a few seconds longer than necessary. Then he gave an almost imperceptible nod. "If you'll excuse me now." The older man turned and left the room.

Olivia smiled at Becker. "One down, one to go—and here he comes."

Romano was heading their way from across the room.

Her smile broadened as Giovanni Romano approached.

His two bodyguards hung back. The older man nodded as he stepped up to the painting, pretending to study it while glancing sideways at Becker.

Olivia tilted her head to one side. "I like it," she said loud enough for Romano to hear.

Romano nodded toward her and turned to Becker. "And you?" he asked.

Becker nodded. "One of my favorites. But then, I love beautiful women. I find the woman in the painting quite exquisite."

Romano's gaze returned to Olivia. "As I see. I'd read that you were touring the Greek islands recently."

Becker's mouth twisted into a wry grin. "I was, until I heard of the opportunity to add a Wyeth to my collection. It was worth an abrupt pause in my vacation."

Romano looked back at Olivia. "And did you feel the same? Was it worth disrupting your tour of the islands?"

Olivia gave the man a cute pout. "I admit, I was a little disappointed. However, the Greek islands will always be there. We can always return. The chance to own an Andrew Wyeth is once in a lifetime. So, yes, I was all for flying back to see what it was all about." She sighed. "I was quite saddened when I found out the painting had been stolen. I do hope it reappears soon." She touched Becker's arm. "I know how disappointed Gunter would be if he couldn't have it. He has the most perfect spot to hang it in his Swiss château."

Romano nodded toward the others in the room. "There are quite a few interested in the whereabouts of the missing painting. I hope it will be recovered soon."

"Me too." Becker's eyes narrowed, and his chin lifted a fraction. "I want it. Money is not an object."

"Money always becomes the issue," Romano said, then pressed his lips together.

"I really don't care who has the painting. I just want whoever has it to know—I'm willing to pay whatever it takes."

Romano nodded.

Becker cupped Olivia's elbow. "Have you seen enough?" he asked.

"I haven't seen the painting of the old man in the window," she said with a hint of a whine.

"Monique, darling, we need to leave now if we're to make our dinner reservation."

Olivia nodded and gave him a smile, albeit a tight one. "I'm ready when you are."

Becker glanced at Romano. "If you'll excuse us, I promised to feed my date."

Romano gave a slight dip of his head. "Enjoy your dinner."

Becker held on to Olivia's arm as he guided her toward the exit of the Wyeth room. In the next viewing area, he noted Salvatore was speaking with a barrel-chested man in a black tuxedo.

As Becker and Olivia passed them, the two men turned, watching them as they walked through the room.

Olivia looked back over her shoulder and gave them a perky smile and a wave.

Becker almost laughed, amazed the woman could still play the part when she had to be tied in knots, waiting for Tacey to text her sister's location.

Once outside the gallery, Trace and Irish appeared out of the shadows. Moments later, the white limousine and the black SUV rolled to a stop in front of them.

The ride back to the Ritz was accomplished in silence. Olivia held her cell phone in one hand, staring at the blank screen.

Becker could feel the tension in her body. He reached out to take her other hand and held it all the way back to the hotel.

Once the limousine slid to a stop in front of the Ritz-Carlton, Olivia and Becker got out.

The limousine pulled away, and the SUV rolled up to the curb.

"Get in," Trace said.

Becker held the back door for Olivia. She got in and tucked her skirt around her.

Becker rounded to the other side and slipped in beside her.

"How was the exhibit?" Trace asked.

"Interesting," Becker responded.

"You can tell us all about it in a few minutes." Trace gave Becker a pointed look in the mirror.

Becker nodded. They wouldn't talk about the event until they were out of the vehicle.

"Are you hungry?" Trace asked.

"Starving," Irish responded, rubbing his belly with a grin. "Standing around for hours has a way of making you think about food."

Trace chuckled. "You're always thinking of food. I don't know how you stay so fit."

"High metabolism," Irish said.

Trace glanced again in the rearview mirror. "Steak sound good?"

"Sounds good to me." Becker turned to Olivia. "Are you okay with it?"

She nodded, her attention on the cell phone as if it were a lifeline to her sister. In a way, it was.

They didn't have to go too far to find a steak house. Once Trace parked the SUV and they all piled out, Trace said, "Give it to us. I didn't want to say anything in the vehicle. It could have been bugged while it was parked in the garage."

Becker nodded toward Olivia. "We had an interesting conversation with Tacey Rogers."

"I assumed you had when Olivia texted her name to us. I had Matt do some digging on the lady. He got back to us pretty quickly."

Olivia glanced up from her phone. "What did he find?"

"She used to date Eduardo Romano. They broke up a couple of months ago but remained friends."

"Apparently, she's still in good with the Romano family even after her breakup," Olivia said. "After a brief conversation with the two of us, she came to me while I was alone and said she knew who we were."

Trace shot a glance at Olivia. "Did she blow your cover?"

Olivia shook her head. "No. She cornered me to say she knows where my sister is, that she's seen her and she's alive."

"Did she tell you where she is?" Trace asked.

Olivia shook her head. "No. I gave her my phone number. She said she'd let me know when she made sure they hadn't moved her from her last known location."

"You realize that by telling you where your sister is, Tacey is putting herself in a lot of danger." Irish frowned. "The Romanos have a way of eliminating people who betray the family."

Olivia nodded. "Tacey has to know that, but she was more than willing to let me know about her. She doesn't like that they're using her as a pawn in a showdown with the Salvatores."

"Is your cell phone fully charged?" Trace asked.

"Yes." Olivia checked the screen again. "It's killing me to wait."

Trace waved a hand toward the restaurant. "We can blow some time eating. It will help take your mind off the passing time. Besides, you need to keep up your energy."

"That's right," Irish said. "When that call comes through, we'll need to be on our way immediately."

"And while we're waiting for our order, you two can tell us about the others you ran into at the exhibit," Trace said.

Throughout dinner, Olivia stared at her cell phone as if willing it to ring. She barely touched the fillet Becker had ordered for her.

Becker gave a detailed account of the people they encountered at the event.

"Any more news on the dark web about any black market auctions scheduled soon?" Becker asked.

Trace shook his head. "Matt's monitoring the web. He said social media sites for rabid art collectors have been passing veiled messages about the missing painting. A lot of people speculate that the piece is already in the hands of the new owner." Trace took a bite of his steak.

Irish picked up where Trace left off. "Nico wasn't arrested until the following day. That would have given him time to pass the painting to whoever he had in mind to sell it to."

"Or to stash it somewhere until the authorities had time to process the murder scene and the body Nico hadn't had the time or inclination to dispose of," Becker suggested.

"He didn't know when he left the scene that my sister had been there and witnessed the murder," Olivia said. "He might have been more concerned about establishing his alibi in case the police came looking for him."

"No matter who has the painting or where it is, we've confirmed the Romanos have Olivia's sister," Becker said.

"And the last time Tacey saw her, she was being held in a warehouse in south Dallas near the rail yard," Olivia said. "And she was alive."

"They are keeping her alive for a reason," Irish said.

"The Romanos know the Salvatores have the painting." Becker nodded toward Olivia. "They will leverage Olivia's sister to trade for it."

"The question is," Trace said, "are the Salvatores as mercenary as the Romanos? Will they be willing to give up the prize to keep Nico out of jail?"

"The Salvatores might not have a choice," Becker said. "If Nico is the only one who knows where the painting is, everyone has to wait until the authorities release him to find it."

"The Romanos can't negotiate a trade with anyone but Nico. They have to keep Olivia's sister under wraps until Nico is free. They can't risk the Salvatores killing Jasmine before they know for sure Nico has the Wyeth painting. Nico has the most to lose if Jasmine resurfaces to testify in court that he was at the gallery that night and killed Eduardo."

Trace nodded. "Nico won't want to go back to jail. If he knows where the painting is and his family doesn't, he might be willing to trade the painting for the witness. His family might not be as willing, even if it means Nico goes to jail for life."

By the time they'd finished dinner, Becker could tell the stress was getting to Olivia. "Let's go back to the Ritz."

"Just remember," Trace said, "you can't talk in your room, even if you check for bugs. The Italian mafia didn't get so wealthy playing by any rules or moral standards."

"We'll bear that in mind," Becker said.

"If you need to talk to us, text us. We can meet in the lobby." Trace paid the bill and then pushed back from the table and stood.

Becker rose and extended a hand to Olivia. She was still holding her cell phone in her hand.

Dark shadows were beginning to form beneath her eyes.

He hated seeing her so worried and stressed, and he hated even more that he could do nothing to help take away her pain. All he could do was be there for her and take action when the call came through.

Once again, Becker and Olivia claimed the back seat of the SUV, with Trace driving and Irish riding shotgun.

At the Ritz, Trace hesitated handing the keys to the SUV over to the valet. "Could you park it as close as possible?" he asked. "There's a possibility we may have to leave in a hurry."

The valet arranged to have the SUV parked in the drop-off area throughout the night instead of driving it around to the garage.

Olivia stared at the SUV sitting at the end of the loading-and-unloading zone. "I feel like we should be driving toward the rail yard. We could wait close by for the call."

"What if they've moved her?" Becker said. "To the north end of Dallas?"

"We will have wasted time, and it would take longer to get there from the south side of Dallas." Olivia sighed. "I know. I need to be patient. It's hard."

Becker slipped an arm around her waist.

"We'll move quickly when you get that call,"

Trace promised. "In the meantime, Irish will see you two up to your room. You okay with that, Irish?"

Irish popped a salute and a grin. "Yes, sir." He turned to Becker and Olivia. "Are you going straight up to your room, or do you want to make a pit stop at the bar for a drink?"

Olivia shook her head. "I want to go to our room. At least there I can stare at my phone and people won't look at me funny." She gave him a weak smile. "I'd like a drink, but I need to keep a clear head for when I get that call with the location of where they're keeping my sister."

"I get that," Irish said. "And as much as I'd like a beer, I'll pass."

Trace lifted his chin at Becker. "I'm going to touch base with Matt one more time. I sent a plane to pick them up. I have a strong suspicion we're going to need them soon. Especially if we get caught in a war between the Romanos and the Salvatores."

With Irish as their bodyguard, Becker and Olivia rode up the elevator to their floor and entered their room. Irish went in with them and helped conduct a search for listening or video devices. Once they were fairly certain the room was clear, Irish stepped out to stand guard in the hallway.

"Thanks, man," Becker said before his team-mate left.

"No worries," he said with a wink. "I've got your six." He pulled the door shut between them.

Becker turned to find Olivia. When he didn't see her in the sitting room, he went to the bedroom. It was empty too, but the bathroom door was closed.

Moments later, Olivia came out, wearing black slacks and a black blouse. She'd pulled her hair back in a ponytail and wore matching flat shoes. "I'd rather be in my jeans and a T-shirt, but at least I have these." She nodded toward his suitcase. "You might want to change into something less fancy. When we get the call, we won't have time to change."

He crossed the room to her and gathered her in his arms. "I love that when you're crazy worried, you hold it together." He kissed her forehead. "I'll be out in a minute."

Becker gathered slacks, a dark polo shirt and a leather jacket before disappearing into the bathroom. Less than five minutes later, he was ready to go.

As he emerged from the bathroom, he heard the ping of a text message coming across on Olivia's cell phone.

He hurried out to the sitting area, where he

found Olivia staring down at the screen, her eyes wide, her face pale.

"Is it her?" he asked.

She nodded. "She sent a GPS pin." Without waiting for his response, Olivia spun and ran for the door.

Becker hurried to keep up.

When they burst out into the hallway, Irish asked, "You get the call?"

"Yes." Olivia didn't slow down until she reached the elevator. She paced as she waited for the door to open.

On the way down, Irish sent a text to Trace.

By the time they emerged into the lobby, the SUV was waiting for them out front.

Olivia handed her cell phone to Irish, who brought up the directions. Within minutes, they were on the major highway, speeding through the city, heading south toward the rail yard.

Becker prayed they'd get there in time to find Olivia's sister safe and sound—and that they weren't being led into a trap.

Chapter Eleven

Olivia sat in the back seat, perched on the edge, looking over Irish's shoulder at the map on her cell phone. Ten minutes had passed, and according to the app, they were halfway to their destination.

Becker laid a hand on her back. He didn't say anything, but he was there. And that made Olivia feel a little better. She wouldn't be all right until her sister was safe and away from the Romanos.

Trace glanced in the rearview mirror. "There's a 9 mm Glock under your seat. Irish and I have weapons as well."

Becker reached for the case beneath his seat and removed the gun from inside. He checked the magazine and slid the gun into the pocket of his jacket.

The gun should have made Olivia even more nervous. Instead, it gave her a little sense of relief. Knowing where her sister was didn't guarantee they'd free her without a fight. The Romanos would be armed and dangerous.

A shiver rippled over Olivia's skin.

"When we get there, Olivia, you should stay in the vehicle," Trace said.

She was already shaking her head before he could finish. "She's my sister."

"If you go in, we'll be worried about you and not focusing on getting to your sister," Becker said. "It puts every one of this team in danger. We need someone on the outside, watching to make sure no one comes in behind us. We need someone to have our six."

Olivia chewed on her bottom lip. "The last thing I want is for one of you to get hurt. But hanging back—"

"Will be difficult but necessary," Trace said. "With only three of us, we need a fourth to warn us if this turns out to be a trap."

"We have another gun in the back," Irish said. "Have you ever fired a pistol of any kind?"

She nodded. "I have an HK 40 handgun. I got it after my parents died and I was living alone. I practiced with it until I became proficient, and I go every other month to the range for a refresher."

Becker grinned. "I learn something new about you every time I turn around."

"You'll find the other gun in the bag," Irish

said. "It's a little bigger than you're used to, but it's smooth and easy to figure out."

Becker leaned over the back of the seat and snagged the bag from the floor, bringing it up to place on the seat between them. Inside was another case, several boxes of ammo and a bulletproof vest. He handed the vest to her. "Put this on."

She frowned. "Shouldn't you three be wearing one of these?"

"We only brought the one," Trace said. "We'd all prefer for you to wear it."

She frowned but slipped into it and buckled the front clasps.

Once she was in it, Becker handed her the gun. "Familiarize yourself with it." Then he handed her the magazine full of bullets. "When you feel confident about its functionality, you can load it."

She held the weapon in her hand, testing the weight and checking the safety features. She pulled the slide back to check that there wasn't a bullet already chambered. Satisfied that it was very much like hers, she slid the magazine into the handle without chambering a round. She would only do that if the situation called for it.

"We're two miles from the destination," Irish said. Trace pulled off the main highway onto an access road and turned right, heading into a seedier part of town.

"We'll park the SUV close, but not close enough so that their sentries will see it," Trace said.

He slowed a few blocks away and pulled into an alley between two businesses. "We'll park here."

Olivia shook her head. "I'm not staying in the vehicle. Not if it's this far away from you guys. I can't see what's happening to the building where you're headed if I stay here."

"You'll be safer," Becker argued.

Anger surged inside Olivia. "And you three won't." She frowned, her jaw set in a hard line. "I'm going to get close enough to have your back, even if I don't go inside the warehouse with you."

Trace shot Becker a look. "She'll be out in the open. What if someone sneaks up on her?"

"I'll find a position in the shadows with my back against a wall," she said, getting angrier that the men were talking as if she weren't there or didn't have a say in what happened to her.

"Look, I'm here—let me help," she said. "I get it that I'm not trained for clearing a building and you guys must have done it a few times on active duty. But I can handle a gun, and I will watch from a reasonable distance for anyone else showing up on the outside when you're already inside."

"Makes me nervous," Becker said. "But she makes sense." He met her gaze. "Only if you promise not to follow us inside. We could end up shooting you, thinking you're the enemy."

She nodded. "I promise."

"Okay, we're wasting time," Trace said. "Let's move out."

As soon as they opened the doors to the SUV, Olivia smelled smoke. At first, it was only a little bit, but as they emerged from the end of the alley and onto the street, she looked up to see a glow a couple of blocks away. Smoke billowed into the night sky, the lights from the city reflecting off the clouds it formed.

Irish glanced down at the GPS location on the cell phone and looked up again. "Folks, that's where we're headed."

Olivia's heart skipped several beats. Then she was running, her eyes filling with tears, making it difficult to see where she was going. She had to get to the warehouse. Her sister was inside, probably tied to a post and surely scared out of her mind.

As Olivia rounded the corner of a brick structure, she ground to a halt and stared at a warehouse completely engulfed in flames.

Sirens started to wail nearby, and soon a fire engine was rolling up to the front of the building, followed by an ambulance.

Firefighters leaped out, pulled a hose from the side of the truck and connected it to a hydrant.

With a firm grip on the hose, a fireman gave a quick turn of the valve, releasing a gush of water from the other end.

Other firefighters suited up in tanks and masks and headed into the burning building.

Her heart thundering in her chest, Olivia staggered forward and then ran toward the crew working the fire.

Becker caught her before she could reach them. His hands held her in an iron grip.

"Let me go," she said, fighting to free herself from his grasp. "Jasmine's in there. We have to get her out." When he refused to release her, she cried, "Please. Oh, please. She's all the family I have left."

"Sweetheart, I know. And I want her out of there too," he said, his voice shaking. He swallowed hard and continued. "You have to let the firefighters do their job. They're trained and equipped to handle this. If there's anyone inside, they'll get them out."

Olivia knew he was right. Her heart in her throat, Olivia stood back, out of the way, wanting with all her being to rush into the building and bring Jasmine out.

Becker's hand remained on her arm, holding so tightly, his fingers would likely leave a bruise.

Trace approached the captain.

Olivia couldn't hear what he was saying. As

soon as they finished talking, the chief turned and spoke into a handheld radio.

Near the front of the building, a man wearing a full mask and oxygen tank kicked open a locked door at the entrance and stood back as smoke billowed out. Once the smoke had cleared a little, he ducked inside.

For the longest few minutes of Olivia's life, she held her breath and prayed.

Becker folded her into his arms as she watched the door. He whispered over and over, "It'll be okay. It'll be okay."

Trace and Irish stood on either side of Becker and Olivia. It felt like a show of solidarity. They were there for her no matter the outcome.

Olivia didn't feel alone. She was thankful for the Outriders. Mostly, she was thankful for Becker holding her so close. With him close, she could handle almost anything.

The longer the firefighter was inside, the more her stomach churned and the more labored her breathing became. Her chest hurt so much, she thought she might be having a heart attack.

"Breathe, sweetheart," Becker whispered against her ear. "Breathe." He said the words almost as if he needed to hear them himself.

She drew in a breath, let it out and did it again. On the third breath, she gasped.

A firefighter was backing out through the door.

As he cleared the threshold, Olivia could see that he was dragging someone by the arms.

A female with blond hair.

Olivia pressed her palms to her cheeks, her heart dropping into the pit of her belly. "Oh, dear God, please."

She lunged toward the firefighter, only to be restrained by Becker. "Let go of me."

"You'll only be in the way. Let them save her."

The paramedics surrounded the woman and went to work on her.

Tears slipped down Olivia's cheeks. "No, no, no," she cried. "Jasmine!"

The woman was loaded onto a stretcher and rolled toward the ambulance. They started an IV and covered her mouth and nose with an oxygen mask.

The firefighter in charge checked with the medical crew before walking over to where Olivia and the Outriders were standing. "Can you identify her?"

Olivia nodded, a lump lodged in her throat, making it hard to breathe and speak. She managed to say, "Let me see her. Please. I know her."

"Come with me. They're loading her for transport to the hospital. If you're a family member, they'll want you to follow."

Olivia and Becker hurried after the firefighter, approaching the ambulance as the techs prepared to load the victim.

With her fingers pressed to her lips, Olivia asked, "Is she…?"

"Alive?" an EMT said with a tight smile. "Yes. But she's a long way from being in the clear. She's suffering from smoke inhalation, and it appears as if she took a blow to the head."

Olivia reached out to brush back the blond hair from her face. The mask covered most of her facial features, and her eyes were closed… but something wasn't right.

Then Olivia noticed that the woman was wearing a white dress. Granted, the dress was covered in soot and damaged beyond repair, but there was no denying it had been white at one time.

"Jasmine wasn't wearing a white dress," she said. Her eyes widened, and she looked back at Becker. "This isn't Jasmine."

Becker frowned. "If it isn't Jasmine, who is it?"

"Oh, dear Lord," Olivia said as recognition dawned on her. "It's Tacey Rogers."

THE FIRST RESPONDERS loaded the victim into the ambulance, closed the door and drove away.

Becker stood by Olivia as she turned toward the smoking building. His heart hurt for her.

"That can't be it." Olivia shook her head, her

eyes widening. "Sweet heaven… She's still inside that building." Before he could stop her, she ran to the man who'd brought the woman out of the warehouse.

The firefighter had shed his mask and was shrugging out of the breathing apparatus when she reached him. "You can't stop now," she cried. "My sister was in that building."

He shook his head and set the tank on the ground. "My buddy went in after me." He nodded toward another man who was stepping out of similar gear. "I only found one person."

Olivia ran to the other guy. "Please," she begged. "Was there anyone else inside that warehouse?"

He shook his head. "I checked all the rooms. The warehouse was fairly empty but for a few busted wood pallets. No one else was inside."

He moved past her to stow his gear on the truck.

Becker was there for Olivia as her knees buckled. He caught her on the way down, pulled her into his embrace and held her until she stopped shaking. "They tried to kill her."

"It wasn't Jasmine," he said.

"But it was Tacey. She told us about Jasmine, and they must have found out. She did it for Jasmine, and it cost her."

Trace and Irish had caught up with them and stood beside Becker.

"I'll meet with the police," Trace said, "and let them know that she'll need protection in the hospital." He crossed to where a police officer was standing, talking to the fire chief. Already the flames had been reduced; the fire appeared to be under control.

Moments later, Trace returned. "So far, they're treating this incident as an attempted homicide and arson. They will provide Ms. Rogers with protection while she is recuperating in the hospital."

"Jasmine was here," Olivia said, choking on a sob.

"Yes, but she's not here now," Becker said.

"Which means they still need her alive for a trade to get that painting," Trace said. "Matt reminded me in a text that Nico Salvatore is being released tomorrow if no evidence is presented by then."

"He'll find that painting."

"And if he doesn't negotiate the trade... they'll kill Jasmine." Olivia pressed her fist to her mouth.

"We won't let that happen," Trace said.

"How will you stop it?" Olivia demanded. "We don't know where they have her. We need to get to that painting before Nico does. It's the only thing they want—the only thing they'll take in exchange for my sister's life."

"Matt and Levi will be here within the hour. I have a plane flying them up as we speak," Trace said. "Let's get back to the Ritz. They'll meet us there."

Olivia glanced once more at the smoldering warehouse.

Becker's arm tightened around her waist. "She wasn't in there," he reminded her.

She looked up at him with haunted eyes. "But she's with people who would do what they did to Tacey."

"Don't." He pressed a kiss to her forehead. "You have to stay positive. For Jasmine."

She nodded, her brow dipping, her jaw hardening. "We have to *do* something. No more standing around waiting for the Salvatores or the Romanos to make the next move."

Becker turned her around and they started back to where they'd left the SUV parked in the alley. Irish and Trace led the way.

"Hopefully, Matt will have more information when he gets here," Trace said.

"Like where they've moved Jasmine," Olivia said.

"Or where the painting might be hidden," Irish said. "We have to search for both. One might be key to getting the other."

"I'm to the point where I want to burn that damned thing," Olivia said through gritted teeth. "Jasmine wouldn't be in the situation she is now if that painting never existed."

Becker agreed. But wishing rarely achieved results. Intelligence and hard work were more likely to produce a positive outcome.

Once Matt and Levi arrived, they'd put their heads together. He'd worked with Levi, Irish and Trace on difficult missions in the past. With Matt's internet savvy and his former team's tactical planning and combat skills, they should be able to initiate a plan to resolve this issue quickly.

And hopefully, without anyone else being hurt or injured.

By the time they reached the Ritz-Carlton, Matt and Levi's plane had landed, and they were on their way to the hotel.

"We'll meet in the bar since it's still open," Trace said.

They found a table large enough to hold six people in the far corner of the room and waited for the other two men to join them.

Each person ordered a nonalcoholic drink, then discussed the fire and Tacey Rogers in between sips. The only one not talking was Olivia.

Becker leaned close and asked, "Do you want to go up to our room?"

She shook her head. "No. I want to be here when Matt and Levi arrive. Matt has to have something else that will help us."

The two men chose that moment to enter the bar. Matt carried a backpack on one shoulder.

Olivia started to rise. Becker touched her arm, and she sank back into her seat.

"Traffic was heavier than I expected this time of night." Matt swung the backpack off his shoulder and set it on the floor. "Makes me glad I live in Whiskey Gulch."

They all made room at the table for the two men and waited while they ordered drinks and a couple of hamburgers.

Once the waiter left, Trace filled Matt and Levi in on what had happened at the exhibit and the warehouse.

Matt let out a long, low whistle. "At least we are fairly certain they're holding your sister as leverage. It's too bad they took it out on Ms. Rogers."

Olivia leaned forward. "Do any of your folks on the dark web keep up with the Romano mafia? Could they have any idea where they're keeping my sister?"

Matt shook his head. "You'd have an easier time finding the painting than your sister. My sources say the Salvatores are scrambling, searching for the painting as much or more so than the Romanos."

Olivia sat back, a frown denting her brow.

Becker could almost see the wheels turning in her head as she processed Matt's words. Her hands clenched into fists, and her pretty lips pressed together in a hard line. Finally, she looked up and met Matt's gaze. "If the Salvatores are looking for the painting, that means Nico is the only one who knows where it is. What do we know about Nico?"

Matt's eyes narrowed. "He's married, no children. His wife lives at the family estate in Dallas. He has a mistress who isn't a secret from anyone. Rumor has it his wife condones it because the other woman keeps him away from her. Wife gets to spend his money. He gets to fool around. Win-win for both of them."

"Could he have stashed the painting at his home or his mistress's place?" Olivia asked.

"The police are still working on a search warrant. With no witness and no evidence that he was even at the Cavendish Gallery that night, the judge isn't issuing one."

"I'm not a judge and I'm not in law enforcement," Olivia said. "I'd be willing to search the woman's home for that painting."

"That's breaking and entering," Trace said. "It's illegal."

"And so is kidnapping my sister and using her as a bargaining tool for a stolen painting." Olivia leaned across the table, her face intense. "I'll break any rule or law around, short of killing someone, if it leads me to my sister. I *might* even kill someone if he or she gets in between me and Jasmine. The point is, we don't have much time."

Becker understood her frustration. "She's right. If Nico's out tomorrow, he could get to that painting, sell it and put a hit out on Jasmine before noon. For that matter, his own family might want to get their hands on the witness to use as leverage against Nico to get him to hand over the Wyeth."

"What do you propose?" Trace asked.

Olivia lifted her chin. "We need to search the mistress's apartment, Nico's office—any property Nico might have access to where he could have hidden that painting."

"His mistress, Lana Etheridge, was his alibi," Matt confirmed.

"The authorities had to have questioned her," Irish said.

Matt nodded. "They did, and they searched her apartment, where Nico claimed to have been all that night. He even produced video from the security system showing him arriving early that evening and leaving the next morning."

"Were there any gaps between the time he came and the time he allegedly left?" Becker asked.

Matt shook his head. "No gaps or erasures. But the video only captures the door entrances, not the windows, which was noted in the investigation. Still, they don't have any evidence he was at the gallery, because the security system was deactivated before Eduardo entered the building."

"Someone had access to the computer system from a remote location?" Irish asked.

Matt nodded. "The preliminary findings indicate a hacker got in and disabled the alarms. Eduardo was able to walk right in and take the painting, and he would have made it out if Nico hadn't arrived first. It would have been a clean heist."

"For either man, except my sister forgot something in her office and returned in time to witness the murder." Olivia placed both hands on the table. "Where does this Lana Etheridge live? The police might have missed something. Or Nico might have hidden the painting in a shed, attic or a secret panel in the floor."

"It would make more sense for him to hide it in a storage unit or an office-supply closet."

"It could be anywhere," Levi said.

"Then the sooner we start looking, the sooner we find it," Olivia said. "I'll check out

Lana's place." She met Matt's gaze. "I'll need the address."

Matt glanced from Trace to Becker and back to Trace. "Are we doing this?"

Trace shrugged. "We don't have anything else to go on."

Matt nodded. "Nico is involved in a building project in the downtown area not far from the Cavendish Gallery. It is possible he could have swung by there, dropped the painting at the mobile office unit. No one is there at night, and he could have had a key to it since he's reported to have been working closely with the engineer."

Levi raised his hand. "I can check it out."

"Any chance he would have taken it by the Salvatore estate?" Becker asked.

"The detective on the case reviewed the videos of vehicles coming in and out, as well as people entering the house that night. That place has cameras everywhere." Matt shook his head. "No sign of Nico and no gaps in time on any of the videos."

"He had to be scared after killing Eduardo," Trace said. "Stealing is one thing. Murder is another, with greater consequences if caught. I doubt he went anywhere with cameras, and even then, since he ended up at his mistress's place, he knew where the cameras were and avoided them altogether."

"So we need to look for places he could have hidden the painting that don't have video cameras."

"We might be shooting in the dark," Olivia said, "but it's better than sitting around doing nothing."

A pinging sound came from her pocket. Olivia frowned and pulled out her cell phone. She glanced at the screen, and her face paled.

Becker rose to stand next to her, peering over her shoulder to read the message. "Who's it from?"

Olivia frowned. "Tacey's cell phone." She stared at the words and then handed him the phone. "We have to do something. Now."

Becker read the words aloud.

"'I don't know who you are, and I don't care what happens to the girl. But maybe you do. Whoever gets the painting to me, gets her.'"

Becker's gut clenched. "We all know Tacey didn't send that text. Romano has it and is using you to get what he wants. That settles it for me." Becker looked up, his eyes meeting Trace's. "I'll go with Olivia."

"I'm with Levi," Irish said.

"Matt and I will continue to monitor the internet and look for other sites close to the Cavendish Gallery where Nico could have hidden that painting. If we find something interesting, we'll head there. Keep in touch." Trace paused, his brow furrowing. "And whatever you do… don't get caught."

Chapter Twelve

"Phone on silent," Becker said as they climbed out of the SUV a block away from Lana's home on a quiet street in a decent neighborhood.

Olivia verified she had turned off the sound on her cell phone. No need for a calling card. Lana could be home alone, with a gun tucked beneath her pillow.

Thankfully, it wasn't a gated community. Nico might be paying her rent, but he hadn't gone overboard with security. Perhaps he thought the security system was enough to keep his ladylove safe.

And from what Matt had indicated, the cameras only focused on the main entrances to the home.

Becker and Olivia approached the residence, clinging to the shadows of the other buildings along the street.

When they were within a few yards, Becker

stopped and held out a hand, blocking Olivia from going farther until he could recon the area.

"There it is." He pointed to a modest brick home that had probably been built in the nineties. The front entrance had a small covered porch.

Nothing about the house screamed *murderer*—or *hiding place for a priceless work of art*—but then again, Olivia hadn't expected it to.

"Let's move around the back," he whispered. "There has to be a window Nico could get in and out of that's out of view of the cameras."

"Did Matt mention dogs?" Olivia asked.

"I'm betting since he didn't mention them, there aren't any. The authorities reviewed the videos. If there had been barking dogs, that would have been an indication of someone entering the house."

Olivia hoped he was right. Guns and dogs were deal breakers. She almost snorted. Like she knew the best methods of safely breaking and entering the home of a murderer.

A tremor rippled down her spine.

She'd never committed a crime in her life. Her parents had raised her to respect the law and the authorities. Yet here she was, ready to commit one and drag a good man into it with her. "Look," she said. "You don't have to go in with me. If I get caught, it'll just be on me. I don't want you to pay for my crime."

He frowned at her. "Sweetheart, I'm not letting you go in there without me. We don't know if Lana is home or if she's armed. What would you do if she pointed a gun at you?"

Olivia shrugged. "Try to talk her out of shooting me?"

"Before or after she pulls the trigger? A lone woman with a mafia boyfriend might shoot first. And she'd have every right to, since you'd be trespassing in her house."

"Still, it was my idea to search her house. You don't have to go down with me. I don't expect you to."

"Are we going in or not? Either I go in with you or neither one of us goes in." He waited for her response.

Olivia was determined to find the missing painting. "I'm going in. If you come along... well, then, that's on you." She lifted her head in challenge, hoping he'd back down and opt to stay outside.

He tipped his head toward Lana's place. "Then we're going in."

Becker swung wide of the house, looking at it from all angles, judging which side would be best to enter from. Starlight gave them enough light to see where they were going.

Olivia did her best to remain in the shadows. When Becker came to a sudden halt, she nearly bumped into him. "What?"

He nodded toward the garage, where a light suddenly blinked on. The garage door opened, and a small red Mazda Miata convertible pulled out into the driveway and paused until the garage door closed. Then the car raced down the street, disappearing around the next corner.

"That was the only vehicle in the garage," Becker said.

"Wonder why she left at this time," Olivia said.

"Whatever the reason, she might be back soon. If we're going to do this, it's now or never."

Olivia nodded. "Through the window on the west side?"

He nodded. "We want to stay out of view of the cameras and the neighbors." Becker led the way, staying in the shadows of the bushes until they were directly across from the window they would enter.

As quickly as they could, they crossed the open ground and made it to the side of the house.

"What are the chances the window is unlocked?" Becker whispered. He placed his fingers on the window and pushed upward.

Olivia held her breath.

At first, the window didn't budge. Then it moved and rose slowly up the tracks. Before Olivia could protest, Becker pulled himself up and through the window into the house.

He leaned out the window and whispered, "Stay here."

"But—"

Becker disappeared into the house. Time crawled for the minute or two it took for him to get back to where she stood beneath the window.

Then he reached down, grabbed her arms and pulled her through. She landed gracelessly on the floor and struggled to her feet.

The window was to a bedroom that had a wood-framed bed pushed up against one wall, its mattress without sheets or pillows. Piles of clothing obscured the bed, and the rest of the room was filled with moving boxes that had been opened but not unpacked.

"Is the house empty?" Olivia asked softly.

"Yes. We need to make it quick." He looked around the room. "This would be a good place to start. I'll get started on the rest of the house."

Olivia didn't like letting him out of her sight any more than he liked letting her out of his, but they had a lot of ground to cover in a short amount of time. Using a tiny flashlight she'd brought with her in her pocket, she dug through the stack of clothing on the bed, checked under the mattress and looked beneath the bed.

Then she worked her way through the larger open boxes, digging down to the bottoms, finding nothing but knickknacks, photographs, sheets and blankets.

The closet in the room was filled with clothes on plastic hangers and shoes stacked on the floor and on the shelves above. The woman liked her stilettos. She had some in every color and style, including a pair of ankle boots completely covered in rhinestones.

Olivia checked the back wall of the closet for hidden doors but found none.

When she emerged from the bedroom, she almost ran into Becker in the hallway. "I checked the master bedroom. Nothing but a lot of shoes."

Olivia snorted. "Her shoe collection overflowed into this room as well."

"I'm headed for the living room," Becker said. "There's another guest bedroom, if you want to take that."

She nodded and crossed the hallway into the other guest room, which had a white iron bed, this one covered in a floral-print comforter with matching pillows.

Olivia started there, feeling under the pillows and sliding her hands beneath the blankets and sheets. She checked between the mattress and box spring—nothing. She dropped to the floor and slid beneath the bed, checking the underside of the box spring. Other than a few dust bunnies, she didn't find anything.

The closet contained empty suitcases. She checked each one, only to be disappointed when she found that they were all empty. Again, she checked the back wall of the closet for any hidden doors.

The only other items in the room were a dresser, two small nightstands and a print of a spring garden that hung over the headboard.

She checked all the drawers in the dresser and nightstands, even pulling them out to look behind and beneath them. Getting desperate, she lifted the print off the wall and checked the back, but it didn't appear to have been tampered with.

Out of options, she headed for the living room. As she emerged from the hallway, headlights shone through the picture window as a vehicle passed on the street and slowed to a stop.

"Becker!" she called out.

A door creaked from somewhere beyond the dining room.

The vehicle pulled up in front of the little house and parked next to the curb.

Her heart beating like a snare drum solo, Olivia ran through the dining room and into the kitchen. "Becker!" she called out again in an urgent whisper.

He stepped out of the walk-in pantry. "What?"

"A car," she said. At that moment, the rumble of a motor sounded: the garage door was opening. Which meant Lana was back.

Olivia pushed Becker back into the pantry and stepped in with him, closing the door to just a crack as the door between the kitchen and the garage swung open.

A woman carrying a paper bag entered and flipped the light switch, bathing the kitchen in soft yellow light. She left the garage door open as she set the bag on the counter and pulled out four full bottles—two of red wine, one of whiskey and the other of gin.

"Whiskey on the rocks?" she called out and headed for the refrigerator, snagging a glass from a cabinet on the way.

"Sounds good," a male voice responded. A moment later, a man with graying hair, wearing black trousers and a black long-sleeved shirt, entered, pulling a necktie loose from around his throat. He tossed it on the counter and unbuttoned the top button of his shirt.

The woman Olivia assumed was Lana handed him a glass filled with whiskey and a couple of cubes of ice. "Better?" she asked with a smile.

He took a long swallow, downing half the liquid in the glass before responding. "Yes."

Olivia held her breath, praying Lana didn't decide to stow the other bottles in the pantry.

"He gets out tomorrow?" the man asked.

Lana nodded. "Yes, he does."

"Are you sure he'll be back here?"

"Absolutely. He hates his wife. She only stays married to him so she can live on the family estate. She made it clear that she doesn't much care for him, and she actually gets along better with his dad. Nico and Briana haven't lived together for over a year." Lana chuckled. "Since he moved in with me."

"If he comes back here, we'll see less of each other," the man said.

"That means we need to make the most of tonight." She took the glass from his fingers and set it on the counter; then she wrapped her hand around the back of his neck and pulled him down for a kiss.

He dragged her body up against his and deepened the kiss.

She hooked one of her calves around the back of his thigh, her short dress rising up.

"Ummm," he growled. "Let's take this and the whiskey to the bedroom."

She laughed, grabbed the bottle of whiskey and his glass, and led the way through the kitchen and out of view of the pantry. The light blinked off, leaving Olivia and Becker in the dark.

"So," the man said, "Nico didn't tell you where he hid the painting?"

Lana snorted. "Do you think I'd still be in this stinking house or this stinking town if he had?"

"No. I guess not. If I had it, I'd have been long gone."

"I looked all over this house. It's not here. I have no idea where it is. I just hope when he's out and sells it, I get some of the proceeds for being his alibi. Still can't believe he killed Eduardo. He'll be lucky to make his next birthday if the Romanos have their way. Sadly, that would mean I'll lose this house."

Her voice faded the farther away she moved.

A moment later, music sounded from the living room, and Olivia could hear Lana's laugh.

When she started to open the pantry door wider, Becker touched her arm. "Wait," he whispered.

She let her hand drop and did as he'd suggested.

After what felt like an hour—but was probably only ten minutes—Becker pushed the pantry door open and stepped around Olivia and into the kitchen.

He tiptoed across the tile floor.

Olivia followed, careful not to bump into anything in the darkness. Fortunately, starlight filtered through the windows, giving them just enough light to find their way through the dining room and living room.

In the hallway, the only light came from the half-open door to the master bedroom.

Muffled voices rumbled from within. A giggle, an answering deep laugh and silence. Footsteps sounded.

Becker ducked through the door to the guest room they'd come in through. He pulled Olivia in after him and pulled the door to.

The creaky sound of another door broke the silence.

"I'll be right back with my wine," Lana called out. "Do you want anything?"

"Just you, darlin'," the man responded.

Becker and Olivia made their way through the maze of boxes to the window and waited for the sound of Lana returning to her bedroom and closing the squeaking door before making their exit.

"You first," Becker said.

Olivia swung one leg over the windowsill, then the other, and dropped softly to the ground.

She turned and waited for Becker, who soon landed beside her.

He gripped the bottom of the window and pulled it down as far as it would go before he had to place his fingers on the glass and ease it down the rest of the way. Then he took off his shirt and used it to wipe away any fingerprints he'd left behind.

Throughout the process, Olivia watched the room for movement.

A light blinked on in the hallway, shining a sliver of light through the crack in the door.

A moment later, the door swung open.

Olivia grabbed Becker's shoulder and pushed him down below the windowsill.

The light in the bedroom flashed on.

"I thought I heard a sound," they could hear the man say.

"Oh, you're being paranoid. They aren't letting Nico go until tomorrow morning. That is, if that woman who claimed she witnessed him murdering Eduardo doesn't show up out of the blue to keep that from happening. I bet Nico's family got to her. They won't want her blabbing and keeping Nico from getting out to show them where he left that stupid painting."

The window above Olivia and Becker slid open. "Don't you ever lock your windows?" the man asked.

"If I did, how would Nico use me as an alibi?" She huffed. "If it makes you feel better…" The window slammed shut, and the locks clicked in place. "Happy?" Lana asked, her muffled voice moving farther away from the window. "Now, can we have a little fun before Nico shows up?"

Becker touched Olivia's arm, and he tipped his head toward the bushes.

They ran for the shadows, working their way around the yards and back to the SUV. They jumped in.

As Becker turned the SUV around in the street, he glanced at Olivia. "Let Trace know what we found."

"Basically, nothing we didn't know," Olivia said. "And no painting." She pulled out her phone and sent Trace a text.

No painting at Lana's. Lana showed up. Overheard her with another man. As suspected, she's lying about Nico's alibi.

He responded within seconds.

No painting in the office at the construction site. Levi and Irish heading back.

Same. Any other locations we should look?

It will be morning soon. We'll tail Nico when he's released.

Roger.

"We're back to square one." Olivia sighed, her heart aching. "And my sister is still a hostage."

The only thing holding her together was the fact that she was with Becker. He was her rock in this sea of uncertainty.

She glanced at the time on the dash. It was nearly three o'clock. Like Trace had said, it would soon be morning.

Nico would be freed. Everyone would be following him, from the Romanos to the feds. Her sister's life hung in the balance of who got to him and the painting first.

Chapter Thirteen

Becker handed the keys over to the valet and escorted Olivia into the Ritz-Carlton.

Levi, Irish, Matt and Trace rose from the plush seating in the lobby and met them halfway to the elevators.

"We're going to catch a few hours of sleep," Trace said. "I wanted you to know we'll be up early to get to the jail before they release Nico. Levi and I will follow him wherever he goes for as long as it takes for him to get the painting."

Olivia nodded. "You might be wasting your time. He's not stupid. He'll know that he'll be followed."

"I'll be monitoring the internet for any sign of his coordinating a sale," Matt said. "Until he makes his move, we have nothing to go on."

"I know." Olivia's shoulders sagged. "I'm tired. I think I'll get a couple of hours' sleep too. Wake me if you hear anything?"

"I will," Trace said.

Becker's chest tightened. If he could, he'd take all her pain away. To do that, he'd have to free her sister. And that wasn't going to happen without that painting.

"I'm going up with her," Becker said. "I'll be down early for an update."

Trace nodded. "I'm sorry things didn't work out the way we'd hoped at the warehouse."

Olivia nodded. "Me too. Thanks for trying."

Becker walked with Olivia to the elevator. Once inside, he reached for her hand and held it all the way up to their floor and down the hallway to their room.

Once inside, he pulled her into his arms and held her.

She didn't move for the longest time, her cheek pressed to his chest, her arms wrapped around his waist.

He wanted to promise her they'd find and free her sister, but he wasn't sure they would. Not alive, anyway. Not after what had happened at the warehouse.

The Romanos were playing for keeps. Even with the death of one of their own, they would stop at nothing to get their hands on that painting. Including trying to kill Tacey Rogers. If Olivia's sister stopped being of value to them, they'd dispose of her as well rather than go to jail for kidnapping.

Becker stroked Olivia's hair back from her face and tipped her chin upward. "Are you going to be okay?"

She nodded. "It's not over yet. I have to be okay to see this through. As long as she's still alive, I have to fight to get my sister back."

His heart swelled at her loyalty and determination. "I'm with you on this. Whatever we have to do. Even breaking and entering."

Her lips quirked. "Yes, you did. And thank you for being there. I doubt very much I would have been able to crawl through that window so easily."

"Anything for a pretty lady," he said and bent to brush his lips across her forehead.

She tipped her head back and captured his lips with her own. "I don't know what I would have done if you hadn't come into my shop to buy a vase for your mother."

"And I'm still wondering what it would be like to go out on a date with you."

She stared up into his eyes. "I think we're past the first-date awkwardness."

"Maybe," he said. "But we're not past the first date. I'm taking a rain check."

She chuckled. "You're on."

He brushed his thumb across her cheek. "You can have the shower first."

"Thanks." Olivia gathered her clothes and toiletries, entered the bathroom and closed the door.

Less than a second later, she opened the door and caught his gaze. "Wanna join me?"

He frowned. "Sweetheart, I don't ever want to take advantage of you when you're sad."

Her lips twisted. "Then can I take advantage of *you*?" She gave him a tentative smile.

He loved that she could tease when her world was upside down, how she made him feel when she was near.

Becker took a step toward her. "Are you sure this is what you want?"

She nodded and left the door open as she walked toward the shower, shedding her clothing as she went.

With a groan, Becker followed. He couldn't resist the beautiful artist, and he didn't want to. He went into the bathroom, closed the door and joined her in the shower.

They soaped each other's bodies, lingering beneath the warm spray until their skin pruned and the water chilled.

Drying her off was as captivating as washing her. Before he was halfway through, he'd gone well past his ability to control himself.

Becker scooped Olivia up in his arms and carried her into the bedroom, where he laid her on the bed and proceeded to make love to her, slow and gentle. She'd been through so much in the past couple of days. He wanted to relieve some of her stress, not create more.

He brought her to climax before he claimed his own. When they were both sated and sleepy, he pulled her into his arms and held her close for what was left of the night, loving the way she fit against him and how soft her skin was.

He could get used to holding her every night and waking with her in the morning. This was what he'd wanted when he was looking for love.

No.

She was who he'd wanted. Not just any woman to make a family with. He wanted someone who was loyal to the point she would sacrifice her own life to save her sister. Someone who was talented and humble yet independent and confident. Someone who inspired him to be a better man.

He held her closer, breathing in her scent, hoping what they were experiencing wasn't just a passing fling. It wasn't for him. He prayed she could see him as part of her future.

Not wanting to miss a moment with her, he lay awake until sleep claimed him.

MORNING CAME TOO SOON. The couple of hours of sleep he'd managed to get weren't enough but would have to do. Today could be the day they resolved everything outstanding in the case of the missing witness and one-of-a-kind painting.

Or it could be the day everything went to hell. Too many variables were still up in the air for Becker to lie in bed, enjoying the company of a woman, no matter how beautiful she was.

They had to come up with a plan to save Olivia's sister and keep Nico Salvatore in jail.

Saving Jasmine seemed to boil down to finding that painting and trading it for her.

But only Nico knew where he'd stashed it. Letting him out of jail seemed to be the only way for them to locate it.

Becker lay for a long moment, taking in every detail of waking up with Olivia, from how warm and soft she was up against his body to the way she'd draped a leg over his in her sleep.

As much as he wanted to stay with her, he needed to see if Matt and Trace had come up with any other ideas on how to resolve the situation without anyone else dying.

Slowly, he eased out of the bed, careful not to wake her. He dressed in the bathroom and returned to the bedside.

Olivia remained asleep; Becker was glad. She'd barely gotten any sleep since her sister had been taken.

He jotted down a note telling her where he'd be and left it on his pillow.

Then he left the room and took the elevator down to the lobby lounge, where he found Trace and Matt with cups of coffee and pastries for breakfast.

"Morning," he grunted, not quite ready to converse until he'd had his own first sip of hot black coffee. He passed them and headed straight for the bar, where he ordered coffee. Once he had a cup in his hand, he joined the two men at a table, where Matt had his laptop open and humming.

He took a reviving sip and sighed. "Okay, what are we going to do to save Olivia's sister?"

"We need to find the painting," Trace said. "That's all there is to it. Without it, we can't negotiate her release."

"What about taking this to the police?" Becker asked.

"They'd go to Romano, he'd deny any wrongdoing and we'd be in the same place. Romano isn't going to keep her where the police will find her, and he won't admit he has her." Trace tapped his fingers on the surface of the table.

"I got a call from Deputy Jones just before I left my room," Matt said. "She was in contact with the jail where they're keeping Nico. When she inquired about his phone calls, they reported he'd made calls to his lawyer, his father and his wife."

Becker's cup was almost to his mouth when Matt mentioned Nico's wife. "He called his wife?"

Matt nodded. "At seven this morning."

"Probably making sure someone will pick him up when he's released," Trace said.

Becker shook his head. "We overheard Lana Etheridge talking about his relationship with his wife. She said his wife hated him and only stayed married so that she could continue to live at the Salvatore estate." He frowned at Matt. "Lana claimed Nico and his wife had not lived together for over a year."

"So?"

"Why would he call her after a year of living with his girlfriend?" Becker ran a hand through his hair. "It doesn't make sense."

"Unless he got her to stash the painting the night of the murder," Trace said.

"I thought the video cameras at the Salvatore estate hadn't recorded any comings and goings that night and didn't have any gaps in footage," Becker said.

Matt's fingers flew over the keyboard. "I'm looking up Nico's phone records. He didn't make any calls around the time of the murder or even shortly afterward."

"Check Briana's—Nico's wife—phone records?" Becker asked.

"On it." Matt continued to work the keyboard, holding silent for a few minutes before he scowled. "She had a call come in after one in the morning from an unknown number and talked for several minutes. She called that number back thirty minutes later."

"That still doesn't account for the fact she didn't leave the Salvatore estate that night," Becker pointed out.

"Probably because she wasn't there that night. She has a charge on her credit card for three nights at the Hotel Zaza resort spa." Matt glanced up. "She could have met him somewhere for him to hand over the painting."

"Why would she do that?" Becker asked.

"Loyalty to the family that feeds her?" Matt suggested.

"But she hated him, according to Lana," Becker insisted. "She could have turned him in and he would have gone to jail, never to bother her again."

"He could divorce her from jail," Trace said. "And if he did, she wouldn't get to live with the family anymore."

"That's messed up," Matt said. "But then, she might not have a way of supporting herself. Especially if she's become accustomed to the lifestyle."

"True." Becker's eyes narrowed. "We need to watch her. Everyone will be watching Nico."

"When is Nico supposed to get out of jail?"

"I called earlier," Trace said. "They said they would make a decision by nine o'clock this morning if the witness did not come forward."

Becker glanced at his watch. "That's only thirty minutes from now."

"The guy at the jail said they'd make the decision at eight, but they'd be sure to stretch out his release paperwork to make it last all day."

"That doesn't give us much time." Becker glanced across the table at Trace. "I'll stake out Mrs. Nico this morning."

"Who are we staking out?"

Becker turned to find Olivia standing behind his chair, wearing the black trousers from the day before and a cream-colored blouse. The contrast between the blouse and her black hair was stunning. Becker couldn't help staring at this woman, who'd been incredible in the shower and in bed just a few hours earlier.

"Briana Salvatore, Nico's wife," Trace said.

Her brow furrowed. "Why? I thought she hated Nico."

"Maybe, but he's been in contact with her since he's been in jail," Becker said. "And we just learned that she received a call in the middle of the night from a strange number the night of Eduardo's murder."

"You think she might have the painting?" Olivia pulled up a chair at the table and sat down.

"It's a possibility," Trace said.

"If she hated him so much," Olivia said with a frown, "why would she cover for him in a murder case?"

"Family loyalty?" Irish offered.

"Or maybe even more… A *test* of family loyalty," Matt said.

"Are we just going to follow her around and see if she leads us to the painting?" Olivia's glance shot from Becker to Trace and back. "She may never do that. Or she could wait until days or weeks after Nico's release. Jasmine might not have that much time. The Romanos won't want to keep her that long."

Becker drew in a breath and let it out. "Then, if I can get her alone, I'll ask her point-blank if she has the painting."

Olivia met and held his gaze for a long moment. Then she nodded. "I'm ready when you are."

"Let's get a bite to eat before we spend the day sitting in a vehicle, waiting for Nico's wife to make a move."

"Okay, but I don't want to take any chances of missing her going to the painting." Olivia shifted in her seat. "I have the distinct feeling that we're running out of time."

Becker felt the same. With Nico getting out of jail, Olivia's sister was in even more danger than she would be if Romano got tired of dealing with her. Nico would also be after her to keep her quiet about witnessing him killing Eduardo.

If Briana knew where the painting was, they'd just have to get it from her.

OLIVIA AND BECKER opted to grab something to eat on the road at a fast-food restaurant rather than wait for a full-service meal that could take over an hour at the Ritz. Matt had given them the address of the Salvatore estate.

With no other clues as to the location of the painting or her sister, Olivia was ready to pull her hair out.

While she and Becker followed Briana Salvatore, Irish and Levi would watch Romano and follow him, hoping he would lead them to Jasmine.

Matt and Trace would follow Nico as his situation unfolded. So far, the authorities holding him were dragging their feet, processing "release" paperwork, which was both buying them time to find Jasmine and slowing them down on locating the painting.

What they had to keep in mind was that Nico may not need or want to dig up the painting anytime soon. He could sit on it for days, months or even years.

Olivia's heart sank to the pit of her belly at the thought of Jasmine languishing in whatever prison in which the Romanos had incarcerated her. She wouldn't give up on finding her sister. She just hoped the Romanos wouldn't give up on trying to make the trade for the painting.

Nico and his family would be searching for Jasmine as well, knowing Nico would go back to jail should she resurface. He would be less likely to bring the painting out of hiding to sell until he guaranteed her silence.

Killed her.

Olivia sat in the SUV beside Becker, her hands clasped in her lap to keep them from shaking.

Becker sat calm, cool and collected, as if he did this kind of thing on a daily basis.

Staking out thieves, fighting bad guys and searching for missing witnesses weren't on Olivia's résumé, nor did she want them to be. She'd led a pretty sheltered life with her artist parents, living in a small town, quietly throwing pottery that sold worldwide.

She'd gladly go back to that life as soon as she found her sister and brought her home safely. Maybe she'd convince Jasmine to stay in Whiskey Gulch and pursue her own artistic medium.

She'd been quite good at painting with acrylics, oils and watercolors.

Perhaps she'd meet and fall in love with one of Trace Travis's Outriders, if he hired any more, as opposed to any of the men she'd grown up with. Life didn't have to be boring in Whiskey Gulch.

Heck, Olivia could *use* a little boredom after all that had happened in the past few days.

Becker had pulled off onto a rutted, overgrown farm road less than a tenth of a mile past the gated entrance leading into the Salvatore estate. He'd driven a mile past the gate before concluding it was the only logical entry and egress to the property situated north of Dallas in the ever-expanding suburbs.

Matt had tapped into Briana's most current cell phone records and determined she was still at the estate. She had also received another call from the jailhouse where Nico was being held.

With nothing else to do but wait and watch, Olivia glanced over at Becker. "I bet you didn't expect your first assignment as an Outrider to fall in your lap."

He chuckled. "I didn't expect the first woman I met in Whiskey Gulch to be so pretty, even when she was up to her elbows in mud."

A smile tugged at the corners of her lips. "All because you wanted to find a gift for your mother. I found that to be incredibly sweet. I hope she likes the vase."

"I loved it. The colors were what drew me to that particular piece." He glanced at her. "My mother had mentioned how beautiful your work was when she visited the Cavendish Gallery. She was right. You're very talented."

Her cheeks heated. As a lone artist working in a small town, she didn't often hear the words of praise that validated her creations. Sales helped, but words in person were even better. Coming from Becker...they were special. "Thank you."

"Where did you learn how to make pottery?" he asked.

"My parents," she answered. "Sort of. My mother painted in oils and acrylics. My father was a sculptor. I learned to love clay from him. He used a kiln for his work, and one day he bought a larger kiln that came with a pottery wheel. He gave me the older, smaller kiln." Olivia smiled at the memories. "When I asked about the wheel, my father got it out, dusted it off and taught himself how to throw pots so he could teach me."

"How old were you?"

"It was around my eighth birthday. He'd sit behind me and hold my hands around the clay, showing me how to work it while the wheel turned. The man had the patience of a saint. I would get frustrated when the pot was bottom-heavy or misshapen. He encouraged me to practice often. On my birthday, he gifted me with twenty-five pounds of clay, five different kinds of glazes, throwing tools and a monogrammed apron." She grinned. "The rest is history. I've even started sculpting. Since my father and mother died, I felt like I should carry on some of the family traditions."

"No painting?" Becker asked.

She shook her head. "Jasmine inherited that skill. She's really good too. Like Mom."

"Why did she work as a curator instead of an artist?"

Olivia shrugged. "She loves art of all kinds and loves discovering new artists and bringing their work to the attention of collectors." Her mouth twisted. "And they don't call them 'starving artists' for nothing. To survive as an artist, you practically have to sell your soul to make enough to pay rent. She works as a curator to pay the bills and paints in oils and watercolors in her spare time. It helps that she really loves her job and meeting people. She was always the more outgoing sister." Her smile faded. "I hope this doesn't change that about her."

Becker reached across the console for one of

Olivia's hands. "You'll be there for her, as you have been all along."

She nodded. "I wish she'd move back to Whiskey Gulch, where I can keep an eye on her." Olivia looked over at him. "Is that being too overprotective? As the older sister, I feel like it's my responsibility to look out for Jasmine now that my folks are gone."

"It's natural to want to protect your family. And family can be more than just blood relations." He looked out the window at the gate to the Salvatore estate. "I'd do anything for my brothers in arms. They've been there for me and had my back on a number of occasions."

"As I'm sure you've had theirs," Olivia added quietly.

"When Trace left the Deltas to take over the family ranch, it felt as if we'd lost one of our own. Irish followed shortly afterward, ready to start a life outside the military. We grieved and were happy for him at the same time. It's hard to have a 'real' life when you're deployable 365 days a year."

"Is that why you left the military?" Olivia asked.

He nodded. "My last mission ended in a helicopter crash."

Olivia gasped and squeezed his hand. "Thank God you survived."

His mouth set in a grim line before he responded. "Yeah, well, that was the problem… I survived with some injuries—but I lived." His tone was harsh and emotionally ragged.

Olivia's heart pinched hard in her chest. "Others didn't," she said. Not as a question but a statement of fact. She could see it in his face and the way he stared into the distance, as if he was looking into the past.

"I pulled my best buddy out of the wreckage, but I couldn't get to the others before the craft burst into flames." His fingers tightened painfully around hers.

Olivia bore the pain silently, knowing what he felt was so much worse.

"Johnny had always dreamed of buying a house on a piece of land, settling his wife and newborn baby there and raising half a dozen more." Becker glanced down at her hand and loosened his grip. "He stayed with me until the medevac helicopter arrived. He wanted me to tell his wife and baby girl that he loved them. He wanted his wife to go on with life, be happy, marry again and have more babies. She was a wonderful mother who needed to have lots of kids to love. He made *me* promise to live life to the fullest and not wait for retirement to be happy."

Olivia nodded. "You never know when your

number is up," she whispered. "I learned that from the death of my parents. They'd been saving for a long time to go on a trip to Peru. They'd wanted to see the ruins at Machu Picchu and visit the museums where they'd collected pottery from ancient civilizations. I was going to go with them."

"That was Johnny's point. Don't wait. Do the things you always wanted to. See Machu Picchu, have half a dozen children and a house on a couple of acres." He gave her a tight smile. "I was injured and my body recovered, but I couldn't unsee that helicopter on fire, my friends…my *family*…inside."

She looked at his pale face; the lines around his mouth and eyes were deeper than usual. "Is that why you held me back from the warehouse fire? Was that what you were seeing?"

He blinked as if coming back from his memories to where he was now, sitting beside her in the SUV, holding her hand. "I couldn't let you go into that building." His tone held so much pain, it made Olivia's heart ache.

"I'm glad you held me back. You were right. The firefighters were equipped for that kind of rescue. I would have added to their work." She glanced up as a movement caught her eye.

The gate to the Salvatore estate slid open, and

a sleek white sports car drove through and out onto the highway headed into the city.

"Looks like a white BMW sports car," Olivia said.

"Matt said Briana has one just like that registered in her name." Becker shifted the SUV into Drive and pulled out onto the road, maintaining a reasonable distance.

Sitting on the edge of her seat, Olivia craned her neck, fully focused on following the woman to wherever she was going. She could be the key to getting Jasmine back.

Then, when the world returned to normal, Olivia might follow the advice Becker's friend Johnny had given him as he was dying.

Live life to the fullest.

She cast a quick glance toward the man effortlessly following the sports car.

Life could be full and satisfying if she let herself fall in love with a man like Becker. He was nothing like Mike.

Yeah, he sounded like he had PTSD and was in the process of starting over. He might have some baggage, having been stood up at the altar and losing his friends to war—but then, who *didn't* have baggage? Besides, her existence hadn't been all that rewarding. It had been what it was—just existing. Not living.

When she got her sister back and they returned to Whiskey Gulch, she wasn't going to wait to start living her life to the fullest. She was going to cash in that rain check and go out on a date with this amazing man. She wondered if he'd be interested in traveling to Peru.

Chapter Fourteen

Becker had never opened up to anyone about what had happened that night when their Black Hawk had been shot down. Not even to the therapist he'd been ordered to see for the two months following his return to the States.

Why had he spilled his guts to Olivia? She had enough to worry about, with her sister missing and now having to follow a murdering thief's wife around.

Once they entered the metro area—and the heavy traffic always present on the highways—Becker struggled to keep up with the little white sports car. Built for speed and maneuverability, the car had no trouble weaving in and out of the clogged lanes.

The large SUV was a challenge. But, with Olivia's assistance, they managed to keep up with Briana all the way into the city. She continued deeper into the downtown area and finally pulled into the parking garage of a tall building not far from the Cavendish Art Gallery.

Becker closed the distance between the SUV and the sports car, afraid he'd miss her turning into a parking space before he could round the next corner.

It wasn't long before she parked and got out.

The woman wore a black dress that fit her slim body to perfection; a black hat with a broad brim; and a thin, shiny gold belt around her middle. She carried a matching shiny gold purse. She strode into the building in three-inch black stilettos like she was on a mission.

Even before Becker could park, Olivia unbuckled her seat belt and shoved open her door.

"Wait. What are you doing?" he demanded.

"I'm going to follow her in. You need to stay out here and watch her car in case I miss where she goes." Olivia didn't wait for his response. Instead, she jumped out and headed into the building, hot on the heels of Nico's wife.

"Damn," he muttered beneath his breath and backed into a parking space across from the white sports car. He got out of the SUV and hustled into the building after the elevator door closed with the two women inside.

He prayed Briana wasn't armed. She might be getting desperate and paranoid if she really did know where the painting was and had a date with the devil to return it. Nico wasn't above killing to get his hands on the artwork. Briana would be smart to be cautious. She'd have to be two steps ahead to stay alive in the Salvatore family.

Becker entered the glass-enclosed vestibule housing the elevator and watched the numbers from the elevator Briana and Olivia had gotten into climb. It stopped on the eleventh floor and then came down to the fifth.

Becker checked the list of businesses on the eleventh floor and frowned. "The Women's Health Group?"

He read the names of the gynecologists and obstetricians listed beneath.

Becker was glad he hadn't been the one to jump in the elevator with Briana; he would have struggled to come up with a reason for going to the exact same floor.

He went back to the SUV and climbed in. If Briana was there for an appointment, it could take more than an hour before she and Olivia came back out.

With time on his hands, he called Trace to report in. "We followed Briana Salvatore to a building in downtown Dallas."

"Did you follow her in?" Trace asked.

Becker laughed. "No, and I'm glad I didn't. She's visiting a women's clinic. Olivia jumped in the elevator with her. I'm standing guard over her vehicle to make sure he doesn't slip past us."

"Good," Trace said. "Matt and I are outside the jailhouse, along with an army of reporters ready and waiting for Nico's release."

"No sign of that happening anytime soon?" Becker asked.

"No telling when it'll happen." Trace said something in the background to Matt that Becker couldn't make out. "Matt got a text from Irish and Levi. Romano is on the move. They're following."

"I'll probably be here at least an hour," Becker said. "Let me know if anything changes."

"Roger." Trace ended the call.

Becker sat across from the white BMW, tapping his fingers on the steering wheel, wishing he could be a fly on the wall of wherever Olivia was. He wasn't good at sitting still, preferring action to inaction. But he was smart enough to stay put.

If Briana gave Olivia the slip, he'd be there to follow. One way or the other, they needed to corner Briana and get her to hand over the painting. They'd do their best to keep her safe until Jasmine was freed and Nico was caught and sent back to jail.

With so much time on his hands and nothing to do with it, his thoughts turned back in time to when he was engaged and what had gone wrong with that event in his life. He hoped he'd learned enough from that experience to not screw up his next foray into matters of the heart.

He'd never believed in love at first sight... until he'd met a certain artist with muddy hands and spots of clay on her face. She was strong and talented, and she cared about family.

Becker recognized he had a long way to go before he could face another fire without the flashbacks of the helicopter crash. His heart would always hurt when he remembered the friends he'd lost—but maybe, if he took it slowly with Olivia, they could build the kind of love he'd always dreamed of. One day, he might ask her to marry him. And as scary as it might be, he wanted kids.

As an only child, he'd always wanted brothers and sisters, and he'd dreamed of the day when he would have children of his own. He wouldn't stop at one. He wanted enough so that none of them would be lonely.

He wasn't sure how Olivia felt about children. Apparently, she was the oldest of the two sisters. She'd said Jasmine was the only family she had left. He wasn't sure when her parents had passed or how old Jasmine was when that had happened. Had Olivia shouldered the responsibility of raising her sister? Was she tired of being a parent?

She'd talked about the trip to Peru she'd planned with her parents. Was she more interested in travel than settling down to raise a family?

As much as he wanted a family, could he give up the idea if Olivia wasn't interested? He thought about the woman and how much he enjoyed being with her. Yes, he wanted kids. But kids grew up and moved away. If he married, it would be for life. His wife would be with him always. He could see himself growing old with Olivia. If she wanted to travel and see the world, he would travel with her and enjoy every second they were together.

He chuckled softly. "Dude, you're getting ahead of yourself. Relax. You don't want to scare her away by planning the wedding before you've gone out on your first date."

Pulling his thoughts away from dating and marrying Olivia, he went back through everything he knew about the murder, the stolen painting, Nico's wife and girlfriend, Giovanni Romano, and Tacey Rogers. Was he missing any clues?

He hoped and prayed Briana Salvatore could shed some light on the location of the Wyeth— before Nico left the jailhouse.

OLIVIA DIVED INTO the elevator as the doors closed, with no idea of what she might say or do.

"What floor?" Briana asked.

Olivia glanced at the number Briana had pushed and forced a smile. "We're going to the same place. How fortunate."

"I've been with Dr. Adams for the past four years. Which doctor do you see in the group?"

For a moment, Olivia went blank. *Doctor? Group?* She gave Briana a weak smile. "I'm new to the group, and I'm afraid to say—I've forgotten which doctor I have an appointment with."

Briana smiled back. "Don't worry. They'll have it in their system. Are you here for a regular visit or are you expecting?" She held up her hands. "Not that you look pregnant or anything. It's just that so many of the patients here are pregnant, I just assume they're either already pregnant, trying to get pregnant or have just had their babies and are back for a checkup."

Olivia laughed and avoided giving an answer by asking, "Which one are you?"

"For years, I was one of those trying to get pregnant...for all the wrong reasons."

Olivia frowned. "I don't understand."

Briana's lips pressed together. "I thought it would help save my marriage. It took a couple of miscarriages to realize nothing was going to save my marriage. He never loved me and never will."

"I'm sorry. That must be hard, losing a baby and knowing you're losing your marriage as well."

"Yeah, but you can lie around feeling sorry for yourself or you can get up and get on with living."

"That sounds like a healthy attitude." Olivia was beginning to like Nico's wife and was feeling really sorry for the woman married to such an uncaring man. And the fact that he was a murderer—well, that made for a lousy situation all around.

The elevator door opened into the lobby of the Women's Health Group.

"Good luck," Briana said. "I hope your appointment goes well."

"You too," Olivia said. She hung back, allowing Briana to check in for her appointment first. Once she had been escorted back to an examination room, Olivia found a corner to wait and watch for when Briana came back out.

While waiting, she studied the other patients. As Briana had said, many were young women in various stages of pregnancy—from smiling giddily and waving black-and-white sonogram printouts to others who appeared to have swallowed a whole watermelon and could barely get out of the chair to waddle into the examination rooms.

Most were glowing with the expectation of a happy, healthy baby at the end of their pregnancy.

And every one of those women, even those with barely a baby bump, rested a hand on her belly as if reassuring or protecting the life within.

Without really thinking about it, Olivia's hand went to her flat stomach. What would it feel like to have a baby growing inside her? Would she be as ecstatic as most of the women in the room? She'd heard of morning sickness during the first three months of pregnancy—would she be one of the unlucky ones to experience it? And what about those who went into labor too early for the fetus to be viable? Or what if she was like Briana and miscarried, or what if she gave birth prematurely, before the baby had a chance to survive outside the womb?

All the things that could go wrong made the idea of procreating frightening.

But as she looked around the room at the loving smiles as the mothers-to-be looked down at their swollen bellies, all she saw was hope for the future. Of the baby, new beginnings and love.

Olivia's heart swelled. Even when she was dating Mike, she hadn't given much thought to children. She was just beginning to establish herself as an artist, starting to make a little money with her work and renovating the home she'd inherited from her parents.

Now that she was more financially secure, more settled and nearing her thirtieth birthday, she had begun to wonder if she'd ever have children.

Becker would make beautiful babies.

The thought popped into her head and shocked her with how easily it had come. And now that she'd thought it, she couldn't unthink the image of a little boy with shiny blond hair and blue eyes that would melt her soul. Or a little girl with long blond hair and blue eyes. She'd have her daddy wrapped around her little finger so fast…

The woman who married Becker would be very lucky. He was kind, funny, and loyal to family and friends. He'd take care of his own and be there when they needed him most.

What would it be like to have his baby growing in her belly? Her heart skipped several beats as she went over the past two nights with Becker. He'd used protection the first night.

Her stomach churned. Last night, they had been too caught up in each other to think about protection. What if…?

At that moment, Briana emerged from the door leading to the exam rooms. She slipped a pair of sunglasses over her red-rimmed eyes and dabbed her nose with a tissue; then she stuffed the tissue in the purse looped over her arm, squared her shoulders and headed for the elevator.

Olivia jumped to her feet and once again dived into the elevator as the doors slid shut.

Smiling brightly, she asked, "How did your visit go?"

Briana maintained her squared shoulders for exactly three seconds. Then she sagged and buried her face in her hands. "It's impossible. I don't know what I'm going to do." Her shoulders shook with her quiet sobs. "I'm so scared."

Olivia slipped an arm around the woman's shoulders. "You want to talk about it? I'm a good listener."

"It won't help. There's no way out of this mess. None." She pulled her sunglasses off and looked into Olivia's eyes. "And I'm pregnant," she wailed.

"Oh, sweetie. Where can we go to talk? I don't feel right leaving you alone."

"You can't help me. No one can." The door to the elevator opened up into the glass vestibule inside the parking garage.

"You can't drive," Olivia said. "Not in your state. Is there anyone you want me to call? Or would you rather I drive you somewhere?"

Briana dug in her purse and handed Olivia her keys. "Please, take me anywhere. Away from everyone. I need to get as far away from here as possible."

"What do you mean by 'here'? This building?" Olivia asked.

"This building, this city, Texas, this godfor-saken country. I can't get far enough away to save this baby." She looked at Olivia and laughed, choking on a sob. "I don't even know your name and I feel safer with you than with my family."

"My name is Olivia Swann. I promise you I won't hurt you or your baby. Let's go find a place to talk. You can tell me what's wrong, and I'll see if I can help. If nothing else, you can bend my ear for a while." She gave Briana a little smile. "You can start by telling me your name."

"Briana," she said.

"Do you know of a coffee shop? Or, in your con-dition, maybe a smoothie shop would be better."

Briana dug her tissue out of her purse and dabbed at her nose, slipped her sunglasses over her eyes and stepped out of the glass vestibule. "There's one just around the corner. We can walk there and leave the car in the parking garage."

Olivia handed Briana her keys. "Then I won't need these for now. And hopefully, by the time we get back here, you'll feel well enough to drive." She held out her arm for Briana.

The young mother-to-be slipped her hand through the crook of Olivia's elbow and leaned on her as they walked past the dark SUV, where Becker sat behind the wheel, his gaze on Olivia.

She mouthed the words *I'll be back in one hour* and held up one finger, all out of Briana's view.

He nodded and waited until they passed and were stepping out of the garage and onto the sidewalk beyond before he got out of the SUV.

As Olivia and Briana turned to the right, Olivia glanced back to see Becker following them.

She didn't feel threatened by Briana, but being with the woman could be a threat in itself if Nico or any of the Salvatore clan decided to take her out. And they could have come to the same conclusion that she had the painting and were following her, hoping she would lead them to it.

Add in the fact the Romanos were probably looking for the painting, and Briana was definitely a target.

Fortunately, the smoothie shop was inside a mall, not on the street, where they would be vulnerable to a drive-by shooting.

All these thoughts raced through Olivia's head as she walked seemingly calmly alongside the ticking time bomb that was Nico Salvatore's wife, not knowing if or when she should run or duck for cover.

Chapter Fifteen

Olivia settled the distraught woman in a seat at the back of the smoothie shop after they'd ordered fruit smoothies and a plate of crackers and cheese.

"First of all, congratulations on your baby," Olivia said, starting off the conversation. She held up a hand when Briana opened her mouth to protest. "A baby is something to celebrate. Take it at face value." She held up her cup and tapped it against Briana's in salute to her pregnancy.

"I want to be happy. I've known for three months that I was pregnant, but I've miscarried two other babies in the first trimester."

"And you've made it past the first trimester." Olivia smiled. "Your baby has a better chance of making it through the entire pregnancy if it makes it past the first three months."

Briana nodded. "Yes. But it might have been better if I'd miscarried this one as well." She looked away while her hand rose to rest on her still-flat belly.

"Why do you say that? What could be so bad that you'd wish your baby away?"

"I don't want to bring him into the mess of my life."

"Who says you have to?" Olivia grimaced. "I don't mean for you to get rid of your baby. Not at all. I can tell you care and want the best for him. But you don't necessarily have to bring the child into the life you live now. Can't you make changes to your world and make it better for your baby?"

Briana shook her head. "You don't understand. I'm Briana Salvatore. I made the mistake of marrying into the Salvatore family." Her voice became a choked whisper. "Once a member, you're a member for life."

"And by that, you mean the only way out is to end your life?" Olivia shook her head. "You can't think that way."

"I don't see any other way. I'm married to a man who has been accused of committing murder. You know him. His name is all over the news. Nico Salvatore."

"I know," Olivia said. "I understand they're releasing him today." She spoke the words in an even tone with no emotion. Inside, she was screaming and gnashing her teeth, wanting to get to her sister before Nico did. She had to keep cool. Briana was already at the end of her tether. She could drive her little sports car off a bridge, as distraught as she was. That couldn't happen until she handed over the painting.

She *had* to have the painting. She was Jasmine's last hope.

"They're going to release a murderer, and he's going to come after me." Briana closed her eyes and drew in a shaky breath. "I might not get to see this baby born. I might not live that long."

"Do you think your husband will hurt you?"

Briana nodded and then shook her head. "Yes and no." Her hand went to her belly again. "He's already threatened my baby. He'll kill it if I don't do what he says." Her voice caught on another sob. "And when he finds out who's the baby's father, he'll probably kill me as well."

Olivia blinked. That was a twist she hadn't seen coming but should have. Though Nico's girlfriend had said Briana and Nico hadn't lived together for over a year, he still could have gone to his wife, had sex and left to stay at his girlfriend's house.

She bit down hard on her tongue to keep from asking who the father was. "He knows the baby isn't his?"

Briana nodded. "He told me I could keep the child if I did what he said and kept my mouth shut." She pressed her knuckles to her mouth and looked into Olivia's eyes. "And I'm telling you. He's going to kill my child."

Olivia took the woman's hand and squeezed it gently. "No, he's not. Not if we can keep him in jail."

"*We?* How will you be able to help? You don't know what he's capable of."

"I have a good idea," Olivia said. "You see, it's families like the Salvatores and the Romanos who terrorize people to get their way. I know because the Romanos are holding my sister hostage, and I can't find her to free her."

Briana's eyes widened. "The witness?"

Olivia nodded. "That witness has a name. Jasmine Swann. My little sister. She saw Nico murder Eduardo Romano and leave with the Wyeth painting."

Briana pushed to her feet so fast, her chair fell backward. "I can't…" She shook her head. "I have to go."

Olivia touched her arm without grabbing it and took a leap of faith that her gut was right. "Briana," she whispered, "I know you have the painting."

She shook her head, her eyes wide and wild. "No. This can't be happening. No one knows. No one would suspect a wife he hadn't seen or touched in over a year."

"It's only a matter of time before the authorities piece it together, as well as the Romanos and the rest of the Salvatore family."

"I'll deny it." She sank into the chair. "I never wanted to be involved. I should have taken it to the police… I was so afraid I'd lose this baby. I don't want to lose him. He's mine. He's the only good thing in my life." Her voice cracked, and tears slipped down her cheeks. "And he doesn't deserve this." She leaned across the table and gripped Olivia's hands. "Help me. Please. I don't know what to do."

Olivia scooted her chair around and pulled Briana into her arms. "I can help you put Nico in jail for good."

"How? He always has a way of getting out of trouble."

"My sister saw the murder. She will testify…if she can make it to the hearing." Olivia tipped Briana's face up and stared into her eyes. "That's where you can help me, her and your baby. We have to get to Jasmine before Nico does."

"How can I help you do that?"

"The Romanos want to make a trade." She held Briana's gaze. "My sister for the Wyeth painting."

Before Olivia finished speaking, Briana was

already shaking her head. "I can't. He'll kill my baby. He'll kill me."

"Not if he's in jail," Olivia said. "The sooner we make the trade, the sooner my sister surfaces and the courts can't set Nico free. But we have to hurry. They're going to release Nico sometime today."

"I know. He wants me to get the painting to him somehow." Briana stared down at her hands held in Olivia's. "What if they let him out first?"

"Either way, we have to free my sister and protect her. As soon as the authorities know she's alive and able to testify, they will arrest Nico again. We have people to protect her and you, if or when the time comes."

"It won't work. Nico never pays for his crimes. Never." She rubbed her arm. "He beat me so many times, and the police did nothing. I was glad when he moved in with Lana. Glad he left me alone." Her brows furrowed. "He murdered Eduardo."

"Did he tell you he killed Eduardo?" Olivia asked.

Briana nodded. "He told me he'd killed him and he'd kill me if I told anyone or if I told anyone he met with me that night."

"Briana. Will you help me free my sister? Will you help me put Nico away for good so that he can't hurt you or the baby?"

She chewed on her lip, her eyes wide, terrified. "It's the right thing to do," she whispered. "But I'm afraid." Again, she rubbed her arm as if remembering the times he'd hit her.

"If we put him away, he'll never hurt you again."

Briana nodded. "You know that if he's released, he'll come for the painting."

"Yes, he will," Olivia said.

"And he'll come for your sister." She snorted softly. "He won't be making a trade. He'll kill her like he killed Eduardo. And he'll kill the Romanos for trying to take the painting away from him. He says it's his. He wants to sell it, buy an island and move there with Lana."

Olivia's mouth twitched. "He'll be disappointed when she doesn't want to leave her boyfriend to go with him."

Briana's eyebrows rose. Then she laughed. "It would serve him right. He flaunted her in front of me. Nico never loved me. He only wanted me to have his babies and carry on the Salvatore name." Her mouth twisted into a crooked smile. "The joke's on him. It wasn't me who couldn't conceive. His sperm wasn't viable. And he'll be in a rage when he discovers the baby will carry on the Salvatore name. The baby's father is Vincenzo Salvatore." Her chin lifted, and she pushed back her shoulders. "Nico's father is the only member of the family who treated me with kindness when Nico beat me. The only man who doesn't treat me like dirt to be kicked in the corner."

Olivia shook her head, a grin spreading across her face. "You do have a complicated life."

Briana's shoulders sagged. "He doesn't know I'm pregnant."

"Why don't you tell him?"

"Because I don't know how loyal he is to his son. If I help put Nico in jail, will he hate me for betraying the family?" Briana shook her head. "I don't know."

"Briana, either way, you have to keep Nico in jail, or he'll hurt you and the baby. If the Salvatores take it badly, we can get you away from here to somewhere safe for you and the baby. You have to think of the baby now. He's your number one concern. As long as Nico sees you as a threat, he'll hold your baby's life over your head to get you to do what he wants."

"And there's no guarantee he won't hurt my baby anyway. He can't be trusted. He's not an honorable man." Briana chewed on her bottom lip. "You can keep me and my baby safe?"

Olivia nodded. "I know honorable former military men who will lay down their lives to protect you and your baby. But we have to hurry if we want to keep Nico in jail."

"I'm the only one who knows where the painting is. Even if Nico gets out, he won't know where to find it."

Olivia bit back her frustration. Already, another hour had passed while they'd been in the smoothie shop. One more hour closer to Nico going free, and the chance to trade for her sister's life was slipping away.

"Where is the painting, Briana?" Olivia asked.

"I can't tell you," she said. "I'll take you there." Her eyes narrowed. "But only you." She tipped her head toward the front window of the shop that looked out over the mall's courtyard, where Becker sat on a bench, pretending to read a newspaper. "He can't come."

Olivia nodded. "Deal."

BECKER PEERED OVER the top of the newspaper as Olivia exited the smoothie store and marched right up to him.

"She knows I followed you?" He folded the paper, his gaze on the smoothie store in case Briana tried to make a run for it.

"Yes. I'm going with her to get the painting. Just me."

His stomach knotted. "Not a good idea. She could be leading you into a trap."

"My gut tells me she won't."

"*My* gut tells me not to trust any of the Salvatores." He reached out and grasped her hand. "Let me go with you."

She shook her head. "I told Briana I would go alone. It will show her that I trust her."

"And why should you trust her?"

"Because she's pregnant and doesn't want to lose the baby." She leaned close and pressed a kiss to his lips. "Track my phone. I've shared my location with you. But don't follow close enough for her to see you. I'll be okay."

"I don't trust her. Hell, I don't trust anyone with your life." He lurched to his feet and pulled her into his arms. "Olivia, I like you too much to let you out of my sight in this city. Heck, I might even be in love with you. So don't go and get yourself killed."

Her cheeks turned a pretty shade of pink at his words. "You love me?"

"I'm pretty sure. But if that scares you, I can say I like you and want to see where it goes." He winked. "I promised myself I'd take it slow and start with a date."

"I think we're past that stage in our relationship. I think we passed that the first night." She glanced across at the entrance to the smoothie shop.

Briana emerged, looked left, then right, and finally her gaze settled on Olivia and Becker.

"I have to go before she changes her mind. She's terrified of Nico. Can you work with Trace and come up with a plan for the trade? As soon as I have the painting, we need to make it happen. Hopefully before Nico is set free."

Becker nodded. "I'll be within a couple minutes of you. No matter what happens, hold on and I'll be there."

Olivia leaned up on her tiptoes and brushed a kiss across his lips. "It might be too soon—and it's crazy to even think it—but I think I love you too." She spun around and hurried to join Nico Salvatore's wife.

Given how dangerous the mafia family could be, Becker wasn't happy. The love of his life was walking away with a murderer's wife.

He was on his phone, calling Trace, as soon as the two women disappeared around a corner.

Trace answered. "What's happening?"

"Olivia is leaving with Briana."

"Did she agree to give her the painting?"

Becker talked while on the move. "So she said. Briana insisted Olivia go with her alone."

"You didn't let her, did you?"

Becker didn't answer.

"Right. She's a strong-willed woman with a mind of her own. I have one of those too. You have her phone on tracker?"

"Bringing it up now. Olivia wants us to set

up the trade as soon as she gets the painting. She has the contact number, but we'll need to be there as backup."

"If I know the way these guys work, they will want her to bring the painting and come alone," Trace said.

"We can't let that happen."

"And we won't."

"That's right." Becker wouldn't send Olivia in to face the Romanos alone. They might renege on their promise to trade her sister. *And take the painting, kill the women and leave.* "We need to prime the engine," Becker said.

"'Prime the engine'?"

"Give the Romanos a sense of urgency."

"How?"

"Gunter Kraus needs to make an offer they can't refuse, with a time limit. That way, when they get word from Olivia that she has the painting, they're eager to make the trade in a hurry."

"What kind of time limit?"

"Before Nico is released."

"That might not happen," Trace said. "They're rumbling about running out of excuses, and Nico's attorney is putting the screws to them."

"All the more reason to make it happen in a hurry." Becker ended the call and emerged from the mall onto the street. Olivia and Briana were nowhere in sight. He jogged toward the parking garage. As he grew closer, the little white BMW sports car blew out of the building and sped away.

His heart pounding hard in his chest, Becker ran inside the parking garage, jumped into the SUV and raced to the exit. Using the tracker on Olivia's phone, he found her already three blocks away.

He pulled out into the traffic and was forced to stop behind several vehicles stopped at a red light. When the light turned green, the vehicles in front of him eased forward so slowly, Becker nearly ground his teeth into nubs. Two of them turned, giving him the break he needed to speed ahead.

To the next red light.

A glance at the location of Olivia's phone made Becker groan. They'd reached a six-lane high-speed highway and were quickly putting miles between them.

By the time he reached the same highway, they had turned off onto another road, zigzagging through smaller streets until they came to a stop.

He prayed Briana wasn't leading Olivia into a trap. No matter how hard Becker tried, he could not get there any faster. Every time he passed a car, another pulled in front of him, slowing him down. The SUV wasn't a sports car; it didn't maneuver through traffic as efficiently.

By the time he reached the exit off the main highway, Olivia's phone was moving again.

It was headed back the way it had come.

His phone rang. Olivia's number was displayed on the screen. He answered with "Tell me you're okay."

"I am. I have the painting. I'm ready to contact Romano to arrange the trade."

"We're close to the zoo. Meet in the parking lot in fifteen minutes," Becker said.

"We'll be there," she said.

Becker hung up with her and then placed a call to Trace. "Meet us in the parking lot of the Dallas Zoo. Be there in fifteen minutes or less. And give me Matt."

"On our way," Trace said. "Here's Matt."

"Can you patch me through to Romano and mask my phone number?"

"Yup," Matt said. "Give me a second."

Becker turned off at the exit for the Dallas Zoo. A minute later, he pulled to a stop in a parking space far away from other vehicles and shifted into Park.

"You still there, Beck?" Matt asked.

"Roger," he responded.

"Okay, you're on," Matt said. "Romano's

phone is ringing. The caller ID will come up as 'Unknown.'"

The phone rang four times, then stopped. Romano didn't say "hello," "yeah" or anything, but Becker could hear sounds in the background. He knew he was there.

"Gunter here," he said. "I'm leaving town today and want to take the Wyeth with me. Four million dollars if it gets to me before I fly out of here in two hours."

After a long pause, Romano said, "How will I contact you?"

"Don't worry. I'll contact you. Four million transferred on the spot when you hand it over. Make it happen." Becker ended the call and prayed his bluff had lit a fire under Romano to do whatever it took to get that painting.

Chapter Sixteen

Olivia breathed a sigh of relief when she and Briana pulled into the parking lot of the Dallas Zoo.

Becker had given her his location, and he was there, as he said he'd be.

As soon as Briana pulled her sports car to a stop next to the SUV, Olivia was out of the vehicle with the painting wrapped in brown paper and tied with twine.

Becker pulled her into his arms and hugged her, painting and all. "I hate Dallas traffic," he said, and he bent to kiss her full on the lips.

Briana climbed out of the car and stood, twisting her hands. "I'm still not totally convinced I've done the right thing."

"You have. You're saving my sister's life. Between the two of your testimonies, you'll put Nico away for life."

"I hope so," she said. "Whether or not it works, I'm taking you up on that offer to relocate me to start over as far away from Dallas, Texas, as I can get."

Becker took the painting from Olivia's hands and untied the twine. "I want to see what all the fuss is about." He carried it to the back of the SUV, opened the hatch, laid the picture on the carpet and unwrapped the paper.

"I checked it over," Olivia said. "It's the real deal."

Wyeth had painted a naked woman walking away from the viewer through a field of ripe wheat. Her hair was the color of the wheat, and her naked body seemed to be a part of the field. The sky stretched over her head in a steely blue unbroken by clouds.

"It's beautiful," Olivia said.

"Yes, it is," Becker said.

"It belongs in a museum," Olivia said. "Not in someone's private collection."

"That's for the owners to decide," Becker said. "But I agree. It belongs in a museum for everyone to enjoy. The man had talent."

Matt and Trace arrived a few moments later, with Irish and Levi bringing up the rear.

They gathered around the tailgate of the SUV and stared at the painting that would buy Jasmine's freedom.

"Now that we're all here, I need to contact

Romano," Olivia said. "We can't risk Nico being released. I promised Briana we'd keep her safe."

Nico's wife stood back from the others, rubbing her arms as if she were cold. "Go," she said. "Trade that painting for your sister. I don't want to be the only one testifying against Nico."

Olivia turned to the Outriders. "What's the plan?"

"When you talk to Romano," Becker said, "don't agree to meeting him alone. Insist on at least one of us going with you." He held up his hands. "It can't be me. Romano will remember me from the gallery. And you'll need some kind of disguise to keep him from recognizing you as Gunter's girlfriend, Monique."

"I have makeup in my purse," Briana offered. "We can change her appearance with it. I also have a light blue scarf she can cover her hair with."

"That should do it." Trace turned to Levi. "You'll go with Olivia to make the trade."

"Trace, Irish, Matt and I will get there ahead of you and be your backup," Becker said. "Whatever you do, don't give him the painting until you have Jasmine out of their reach."

Olivia nodded, pulled out her cell phone and brought up Tacey Rogers's phone number. She took a deep breath, met Becker's gaze and initiated the call to Romano.

"You still want to trade a painting for my sister?" she said into the cell phone.

Becker's heart swelled at how brave she was. Her voice was steady and her gaze met his, unwavering.

Now that they had the painting and a plan, she was ready to get her sister back. And nothing would stop her.

Becker would be there to make sure both women made it out alive. He wished he was going in Levi's place. But if Romano recognized him, he might spook and leave without the painting and with Olivia's sister. They couldn't risk it. Not when Nico would be released at any moment.

"I have the painting. Do you still have my sister?" Olivia paused. "I want proof of life," she said. "Let me talk to her."

A moment passed.

Olivia gripped the cell phone, her eyes filling with tears. "Jaz, baby. Are you all right? Hang in there. I'm coming to get you. Don't worry about me. We're going to come out of this and laugh about it later." Olivia frowned. "Don't hurt my sister, or the deal's off. Do you hear me? *Off.*"

She nodded. "I'll be there in twenty minutes. And just so we're clear... No sister...no painting."

She ended the call and looked up. "Twenty minutes behind a warehouse near the rail yard. Not far from the one they torched the other night." She gave the address and started for Becker's SUV, where she rewrapped the painting and tied the twine. Then, with the painting in hand, she returned to the others. "Which vehicle are we taking?"

"You and Levi can take the SUV I was driving," Becker said.

Irish raised his hand. "Becker can ride with me."

"We'd better get moving," Trace said. "We want to get there before they do, if possible."

"What about me?" Briana asked. "What can I do to help?"

Olivia hugged her. "You've already done it. Without this painting, we wouldn't have anything to bargain with."

"We'll do our best to get it back," Trace said, "once we have the witness safely in hand."

Briana nodded. "I'd like to go along with you, even if I stay in the car when you guys go in." She glanced around. "I don't know where else to go. By giving you the painting, I've cut ties with the family. They will never trust me after this. I can't go back."

"You can come with us," Trace said. "You'll

need to stay back, out of the line of fire, and lie low while the trade goes down."

Olivia nodded. "You won't want anyone to know you're around. If Romano's people find you there, it will place you and your baby in danger."

Briana snorted. "I get that. The Romanos wouldn't take kindly to having a Salvatore at their party. Even an ex-Salvatore." She nodded. "I'll stay out of sight. I have as much a stake in this trade as the rest of you."

"Then let's make sure we do this right the first time." Olivia lifted her chin. "There won't be any second chances."

BECKER RODE WITH IRISH, following the vehicle with Trace and Matt. They zipped through traffic on their way southeast to the rail yard where the warehouse had burned the night before, almost killing a woman inside.

They pulled into an alley a few blocks from the designated address, got out, and grabbed rifles and handguns.

Briana Salvatore parked behind their two vehicles and got out long enough to wish them luck. Then she climbed back into her car and locked the door. She slid low in her seat so that no one would see her sitting there.

Becker stopped beside her car and waited for

her to lower her window a crack. "Be safe," he said. "If anyone shows up, be ready to drive off."

"I feel like I should do more to help," she said.

He shook his head. "Take care of yourself and your baby."

The men hurried through the streets to the meeting location Romano had specified, remaining vigilant, on the lookout for Romano's men.

With the noonday sun shining down overhead, they didn't have shadows to cling to. The men relied on moving silently and stepping between or behind buildings to avoid being seen by the traffic passing by on the road out front.

When they reached the address, they spread out, circled the block and took up covered positions behind whatever they could find.

Becker hunkered down behind a commercial trash can and waited for Romano to show up with his people and Olivia's sister.

They had only been in position five minutes when a white van drove down the street between two warehouses and turned in behind the building where the Outriders lay waiting.

No one got out of the van. The engine remained running, and the windows in front were heavily tinted. Even in the sunlight, Becker couldn't see through.

Two minutes later, the black SUV arrived, with Levi driving and Olivia riding shotgun.

Becker held his breath, praying Romano didn't gun them down and leave with the painting and no witnesses left alive.

He raised his military-grade rifle to his shoulder and stared down the scope to the door of the van, ready to take down anyone who threatened Olivia or Levi.

As soon as Levi brought the vehicle to a halt, Olivia was out of the passenger seat, the painting in its brown paper wrapped in her hand, her jet-black hair wrapped neatly in the light blue scarf. Briana had worked magic with the makeup to contour Olivia's face, making her appear very different from how she'd looked the other night at the art gallery.

She held the painting in front of her like a shield, probably thinking Romano wouldn't shoot at her and risk damaging a four-million-dollar investment.

The side door of the white van opened, and Romano stepped down onto the pavement. He was followed by four men carrying semiautomatic rifles. They flanked Romano, providing royal protection for the mafia kingpin.

He reached inside the van and dragged a young woman out by her arm. Her wrists were zip-tied behind her back, and her mouth was covered with duct tape.

Olivia stepped forward, her eyes narrowed, her mouth drawn into a tight line. "Release my sister, and I'll give you the painting."

"Show us the artwork," Romano demanded.

Olivia untied the twine and balanced the painting in one hand while pulling away the paper with the other. She turned the image to face Romano. "Send her over."

"We'll meet halfway," Romano said.

Becker didn't like that thought at all. He didn't want Romano within reach of Olivia.

"Show me your hands," Olivia called out.

Romano raised his hands, letting go of Jasmine for a second, to prove he held no weapons.

"Your man can do the same." Romano tipped his head toward Levi.

Levi held up his hands, then lowered them and cupped Olivia's elbow, holding her close.

"In the middle," Romano repeated. He started toward Olivia and Levi.

Olivia carried the painting, with Levi holding her arm, across the pavement.

When they were within two yards of each other, both parties stopped.

So far, so good, Becker thought. But his gut was telling him it wouldn't go down that easily. He didn't trust Romano. He sighted his weapon on the kingpin, ready to plug a hole in him if he tried to hurt Olivia, Jasmine or Levi.

He held his breath and waited for the next move.

"Hand me the painting," Romano demanded.

"Not until I have my sister," Olivia said.

"I'll send her over when I have my hand on the painting," Romano said.

Olivia stepped forward and held out the Wyeth.

Romano reached for it. When his hand was on the frame, Olivia held tight. "The painting is in your hand. Send over my sister."

Romano's eyes narrowed. With one hand gripping the frame and the other gripping Jasmine's arm, he had a choice to make.

Becker hoped the offer from Gunter was foremost in Romano's mind as he made his decision.

With a hefty shove, he pushed Jasmine toward Olivia.

Olivia stepped to the side, maintaining her hold on the frame. "Levi, take her to the vehicle."

"I'm not leaving you," he said.

Becker could have hugged him. His teammate didn't trust Romano any more than he did. He didn't want to leave Olivia alone with him for one second.

"Levi," Olivia said, her tone harsh, "take my sister to the vehicle."

"But—"

"Do it," she said.

Levi pushed Jasmine behind him and backed toward the vehicle.

Becker had his weapon trained on Romano.

Then, with a sudden jerk, Romano yanked the painting toward him, dragging Olivia with it.

She maintained her hold—to her detriment.

Romano let go of the painting and wrapped his arm around Olivia's throat.

Becker swore. He couldn't shoot the man without hitting Olivia. He could kick himself for letting Romano get his hands on her. Knowing how ruthless the man was, Becker should have seen it coming. He should have known Romano wouldn't just trade and be done.

"I know you have your people in position to take me and my men down," he called out. "But before you start shooting, I will snap this pretty lady's neck. Think about it. She is my ticket out of here with the painting. Let us go without any trouble, and I'll put her out on the side of the road, unharmed, once we're safely away."

"Don't do it," Olivia said. "Shoot him."

"If they do, they risk hitting you, my dear," Romano said.

"Shoot me," Olivia said. "That way you'll damage the painting, and it will be worthless."

"You wouldn't do that. It's worth millions," Romano said.

"I don't care what it's worth. It's not worth killing for. You never cared that your nephew died trying to steal a painting. You attempted to kill Tacey for daring to reveal my sister's location. You'd use me to buy your way out of here. Well, I'm not going for it."

Becker held his breath, cringing while his pulse raced through his veins. What was Olivia going to do? Whatever it was, he'd better be ready, because it was bound to make Romano mad enough to kill her.

Olivia, still holding on to the painting, went limp.

Romano adjusted to catch her and keep the painting from crashing to the ground. As he bent over, Olivia planted her feet hard against the pavement and came up sharply, her head hitting Romano in the nose.

He yelped, let go of her and staggered backward.

Olivia tucked the painting against her body and darted away.

When Romano lunged for her, Becker pulled the trigger.

The bullet hit the man in the chest. He fell where he stood and pitched forward onto his face.

His men raised their weapons and turned to take down the threat.

"You're surrounded," Trace called out in a booming voice. "Put down your guns, and you won't be hurt."

When they hesitated, Becker fired a shot at one of the men standing beside the van.

He hopped backward, threw down his gun and raised his hands.

The others followed suit.

With Becker covering for them, Levi, Trace, Irish and Matt zip-tied the wrists and ankles of Romano's men. Once all of them had been secured, Trace called an ambulance for Romano. Becker left his position by the trash can and hurried to join the others. He took the painting from Olivia's hands and laid it on the back seat of the SUV.

Then he turned and gathered Olivia in his arms. "When Romano grabbed you, I lost ten years off my life." He held her close, willing his racing heart to slow.

Engine noise echoed off the walls of the warehouses. A moment later, Briana's sports car raced down the road between the buildings and skidded sideways to a halt. She leaped out, her gaze going to Olivia. "It's Nico. He's free, and he wants me to bring the painting to him. Please tell me you still have it."

"We do. And we have the witness that can put him away for life," Olivia said.

Briana shook her head sadly. "You have to catch him first. He's not going to turn himself in. He has to be lured out with the promise of a big prize," she said.

"The painting." Olivia hurried over to her sister. "We need to set up a trap to recapture him. Jasmine and Briana won't be safe until he's serving life behind bars."

Levi had cut the zip ties from Jasmine's wrists. She eased the duct tape from her mouth, careful not to rip her skin.

Once she was free of tape, Jasmine spoke. "If you're going to set a trap to capture Nico, let me deliver the painting."

Olivia shook her head. "I died a thousand deaths when Romano's men carried you out of the house. Please don't place yourself in danger again."

Jasmine captured Olivia's hands in hers. "I'm not a little girl anymore," she said. "I can make my own decisions, make mistakes and learn from them. Nico lied when he pleaded not guilty to murdering Eduardo. I saw him do it. He should pay for it and be taken off the streets before he kills again. So, please, let me do my part to bring the man to justice."

"No, let me," Olivia said. "We just got you back. You're safe now. I couldn't bear it if you got into trouble again."

Briana stepped forward. "I can't let you do this. He's my husband. *My* mistake. I should do this."

Jasmine frowned. "Who are you?"

Olivia nodded toward the blonde. "This is Briana Salvatore, Nico's wife. She gave us the painting we used to negotiate your freedom. She's also pregnant, so she can't meet with Nico."

Trace shook his head. "Nico is going to expect to see Briana with his stolen treasure. It will have to be Briana who delivers the painting and gives us enough time to surround and capture him. If not Briana, then someone with the same coloring. Briana is a blonde with long hair. Jasmine, from behind, looks a lot like her."

Jasmine smiled at Trace. "Thank you for the vote of confidence."

"Just don't get cocky," Trace said with a stern look. "You know how quickly things can go south."

She nodded, her smile fading. "I do." She turned to face Briana. "Where did you agree to meet?"

Briana sighed. "At a park playground in twenty minutes."

Jasmine shook her head. "He almost got away with murder. I want to see his face when he realizes he's not getting away with it. And all of this over a stupid painting."

Olivia laughed. "I never thought I'd hear my sister call a painting *stupid*. What is it you always preached? Every work of art deserves respect?"

Jasmine—dressed in the same clothes she'd been wearing for days, her blond hair a mess and her face dirty—planted her hands on her hips. "Yeah, yeah. Being held captive for three days can make even the most devout art enthusiast cranky." She turned back to Briana. "I'll need your clothes and a hairbrush. I'd also sell my soul for a toothbrush."

Becker's heart swelled at the happiness in Olivia's face that being with her sister inspired. He wanted to see her smile like that a lot more often.

But as Jasmine traded clothing with Briana, Olivia's smile faded, and the worry returned.

They had to see this through. Until Nico was behind bars for good, none of these women were safe.

Chapter Seventeen

Once again, the team took up positions in preparation for capturing Nico Salvatore. This time, instead of meeting in a deserted alley behind a warehouse, their quarry had chosen a playground crowded with small children and their mothers.

Becker and Olivia sat on one of the benches, holding hands like a young couple in love. On another bench nearby, Jasmine waited with the brown paper–wrapped painting that, although beautiful, seemed to be cursed. She'd cleaned her face, brushed her hair and dressed in Briana's black dress and stilettos. The broad-brimmed black hat shaded her face enough so that Nico would have to be right next to her to realize she wasn't his wife. She had Olivia's cell phone tucked beneath her dress, her hand on the button to record the conversation once Nico arrived.

Because they hadn't gotten the police involved, word would not have reached Nico that the witness had resurfaced.

Olivia's heart raced as she sat close to Becker, leaning her head on his shoulder while keeping her sister in her peripheral vision, praying she'd be all right. She hadn't lost her once just to lose her again.

A man dressed in gray trousers and a white polo shirt approached Jasmine.

Olivia stiffened, recognizing Nico Salvatore from the pictures plastered all over the news. "Here we go," she whispered.

They were close enough to hear a little but not all. Olivia hoped it would be enough to know when to step in.

Trace said he'd wait until five minutes before the appointed time to call the detective in charge of the murder investigation. By now, he would have shared the news that the witness was alive and ready to talk. He'd have passed along the address of where they could find Nico to return him to jail. He asked them to come in with sirens off to keep from scaring the children.

Olivia worried about the children. If Nico got spooked, he might take one as a hostage.

Becker had assured her he wouldn't let that happen, and he wouldn't let Nico harm or abduct Jasmine. Olivia believed he'd do his best.

But sometimes the best wasn't good enough—bad things happened anyway.

Nico walked right up to the bench where Jasmine was sitting, her legs crossed at the ankle, her hat pulled low to hide her face.

With her heart in her throat, Olivia watched.

The murdering thief sat next to Jasmine and took her left hand in his.

"You're not wearing my ring," he said.

Olivia froze. They'd thought of the clothes, shoes, hat and hair, but they hadn't thought of the wedding ring.

Jasmine only had to keep him long enough for the detective to arrive and arrest him again. If he happened to say something incriminating, all the better. Their main goal was to lure him out, have him take the painting and get caught with it.

Trace would work with the detective to get Briana a plea bargain: her testimony in exchange for the court overlooking her part in hiding the stolen painting.

"What happened to us?" he asked.

Olivia held her breath, praying Nico wouldn't recognize the difference in his wife's voice. Jasmine had practiced a few times to get the pitch and inflections right. Would it be enough?

"A marriage can't survive on lies," Jasmine

said. "And it won't last if one partner abuses and threatens to kill the other."

Nico stiffened. "I only did what I had to. It was the only way I could get you to listen."

"No one deserves to be beaten the way you beat your wife."

"What's wrong with you? You never talked back to me."

"Maybe I've changed. Maybe I don't want to be married to a murderer," Jasmine said.

Becker's muscles tensed, ready to spring into action.

Across the playground, Olivia saw several dark sedans park along the curb.

Men in casual slacks and blazers got out and moved in.

The bench Jasmine had chosen was facing the playground equipment. Nico would have to turn to the side to see the men moving in on him.

He didn't. Instead, he laid his hand on the brown paper packaging. "Ed wasn't supposed to fight back. He wasn't a fighter. His family made him use his technical skills to disarm the gallery and steal that painting. They had questioned his loyalty. They told him it was his way of proving himself to the family. He didn't want to steal that painting. Or so I was told. I expected him to hand it over. When he didn't, I was forced to take it from him."

"No one forced you to take anything, Nico. You killed Eduardo in cold blood and took the painting."

"It doesn't matter. They have no evidence and no witnesses to prove anything." He stood up, taking the painting in his hands.

"I never should have helped you hide the painting."

He scoffed. "You're weak. When I asked you to marry me, you said you wanted children. And what have you given me? Nothing. Now you're pregnant, and it isn't even mine. All I had to do was threaten the bastard, and you crumbled. You're weak and unfaithful. I should kill you for carrying another man's child. You've tainted the Salvatore name."

"No—you, Nico," a voice said from behind the bench where Nico and Jasmine were. "*You* tainted the Salvatore name when you murdered Eduardo."

Nico spun around to face his wife, a frown creasing his brow. She wore Jasmine's dirty clothes, but there was no denying she was Briana Salvatore.

Becker and Olivia sprang to their feet, ready to come to Jasmine's defense.

"What's going on?" Nico demanded. "Who is this?" He whipped the hat from Jasmine's head and glared at her. "Who the hell are you?"

She rose to her feet and walked around the back of the bench, putting distance between her and Nico before answering. "I'm the witness."

His face burned a bright red, and he lunged for Jasmine.

The bench kept him from reaching her.

Becker grabbed him from behind before he tried to go over it. Nico struggled but was no match for Becker's strength.

Jasmine took the painting from him and handed it to the detective, who'd arrived in time to see Nico lunge for Jasmine. He snapped cuffs onto Nico's wrists and read him his Miranda rights. "But you already know them, don't you? And now that we have our witness and the missing painting, you won't be seeing the light of day for a long time."

"You've got nothing on me," Nico said. "It's my word against hers."

Jasmine held up the cell phone and replayed the recording of Nico confessing to the murder.

Nico cursed as the detective led him away. Another detective took the cell phone as evidence and thanked Jasmine for her part in helping to keep Nico Salvatore behind bars.

She tipped her head toward Olivia and the men of the Outriders. "Don't thank me—thank them. They didn't give up on me."

Olivia wrapped her arms around her sister

and hugged her tight. "I would never give up on you. You're my family."

Jasmine shook her head. "How could the concept of family have such different meanings?"

Olivia shook her head too. "I don't know, but I'm glad *my* family is back." She hugged her sister again, her gaze going to the man standing nearby. The man who'd come to mean so much to her in such a short amount of time. A man who could easily become family, if she let him and if he was willing.

"Let's go home," she said, her words meant for Jasmine and Becker.

Jasmine climbed into the SUV.

Olivia waited beside the vehicle for Becker to finish talking to the detectives. When he finally joined her, she stood in front of him, a frown pulling her eyebrows low.

"What's wrong?"

"Does this mean your job is done?"

"This one is," he said. "I'm sure Trace has more work for me."

"So you'll be staying in Whiskey Gulch?"

He nodded and then frowned. "Do you want me to?"

Her face split open in a grin. "Yes. I do. We have yet to have our first date."

"I thought you said we'd moved way past a first date." He pulled her into his arms and stared down into her eyes. "I think what we're trying to say is, are we game for more? My answer is yes, yes and yes." He emphasized each *yes* with a kiss. "I told you not too long ago that I think I love you. I want to explore that thought until I know for sure."

"Good. I'm all in on this exploration. But I see no need to take it slow. I'm pretty sure I have all the data I need to make a decision sooner rather than later to take *I think I love you* all the way to *I know I love you.*"

He brushed the hair away from her forehead and pressed a kiss there. "I concur. Now, let's go home."

Epilogue

"Did you get more nails at the hardware store?" Olivia called out as she emerged from the kitchen, carrying a tray of drinks for the men and women who'd converged on her house to help rebuild the walls.

"Got 'em," Becker answered.

She'd had to wait to rebuild until she could get the insurance adjuster out and then order the needed supplies to replace the windows and repair the siding.

"Where do you want me to put the sandwiches?" Jasmine asked, lugging a tray full of chicken-salad sandwiches out to the front of the house, where several picnic tables had been placed.

"On one of the tables," Olivia said. "Doesn't matter which."

Becker climbed the new wooden porch steps, took the tray of drinks from Olivia's hands and carried it out to the tables. "No alcohol until the work is done," he said to his teammates.

The Outriders groaned and laughed.

"I can't thank you all enough for coming to help. It will be nice to have the hole in my house closed up before the next rain."

Becker climbed the porch again and pulled her into his arms. "They love any excuse to have a party. That, and I promised steaks and beer when the last nail is hammered in and the wall is complete."

"In other words, eat your snack and get to work," Irish said. "There's a steak with my name on it, just waiting to hit the grill." He grabbed Tessa around the middle and kissed her soundly. "We have the medical staff here in case someone steps on a nail or smashes a finger or toe."

She swatted his arm. "I'm pretty handy with a hammer too. I've been looking forward to this for weeks."

"Me too," Lily said. "Hammering is a great way to work out my frustrations."

Trace caught her from behind. "What could possibly frustrate you?"

She laughed. "You." She kissed him, grabbed half a chicken sandwich and danced away.

Levi helped Dallas buckle a tool belt around her slim waist.

"I heard they set the date for Nico's trial for three months from now," Dallas said.

"That's right," Becker said. "Olivia and I will be with Jasmine when we head back to testify."

"Did I tell you I heard from Briana?" Olivia picked up one of the sandwiches and carried it with her to sit beside Becker at one of the tables. "She decided to stay at the Salvatore estate."

"What?" Jasmine frowned. "Why would she do that?"

"So the baby could grow up with a father," Olivia said.

"Are you ever going to tell us who the father is?" Jasmine asked.

Olivia nodded, happy for her friend and the way things were working out. "The baby's father is Vincenzo Salvatore."

"Nico's father?" Aubrey exclaimed.

"I could have told you that," Matt said.

Aubrey lightly slapped his arm. "Then why didn't you?"

He shrugged. "Wasn't my business."

Aubrey huffed. "Men."

Rosalyn smiled across the table at Olivia. "You've been grinning nonstop since we got here. You look happier than I've ever seen you, and your face is practically glowing. What's up?"

Olivia's cheeks heated, and she cast a shy glance toward Becker.

He shook his head, a smile tugging at his lips. "You might as well tell them. You can't keep a secret to save your life." He held out his hand.

Olivia placed her hand in his. "We're going to have a baby."

Jasmine leaped up from the table. "How? When?" She spun around with a smile splitting her face. "I'm going to be an aunt?"

Olivia laughed. "*How?* The usual way. *When?* In eight months—and yes, you're going to be an aunt."

Becker leaned over and kissed Olivia and then raised her left hand so everyone could see the diamond solitaire on her ring finger. "And you're all invited to the wedding. She said yes."

"And when will *that* be?" Jasmine rolled her eyes. "I'm your sister. I should have known all this."

"We haven't picked a date yet, but the sooner, the better." Olivia laughed. "I want to fit in a wedding dress."

"We can have it out at the Whiskey Gulch Ranch," Rosalyn offered. "How's a month from now?"

Becker frowned. "That long?"

Olivia squeezed his hand. "That sounds perfect."

"I thought you didn't want to take it slowly." Becker brought her hand up to his lips and kissed the backs of her knuckles.

"Are you kidding?" Jasmine threw her hands in the air. "A month is barely enough time to find a wedding dress. Then there's the music, catering, florals, bachelorette party, showers... Good Lord. A month isn't enough."

"I don't care if we get married in jeans and a T-shirt in front of a justice of the peace, as long as she shows up and says 'I do.'" Becker grinned.

"I'll be there," Olivia said. "I've found the right one for me. Nothing could keep me away."

"That goes for me too."

"Then why wait?" Olivia turned to Rosalyn. "Could we move that date up to next weekend?"

Rosalyn laughed. "Of course."

Becker kissed Olivia and turned to his brothers. "You heard the lady. Wedding's next weekend."

A cheer went up around the tables.

"That doesn't mean you get to break out the beer yet," Becker warned. "We still have work to do. We have to have a place to live." He pulled Olivia into his arms. "I love you, Olivia Swann. I can't wait to make you my wife."

"And I love you, Becker Jackson. I can't wait to start the rest of our lives together."

* * * * *

Get 4 FREE REWARDS!

We'll send you 2 FREE Books plus 2 FREE Mystery Gifts.

FREE Value Over **$20**

Both the **Harlequin® Desire** and **Harlequin Presents®** series feature compelling novels filled with passion, sensuality and intriguing scandals.

YES! Please send me 2 FREE novels from the Harlequin Desire or Harlequin Presents series and my 2 FREE gifts (gifts are worth about $10 retail). After receiving them, if I don't wish to receive any more books, I can return the shipping statement marked "cancel." If I don't cancel, I will receive 6 brand-new Harlequin Presents Larger-Print books every month and be billed just $6.05 each in the U.S. or $6.24 each in Canada, a savings of at least 10% off the cover price or 6 Harlequin Desire books every month and be billed just $4.80 each in the U.S. or $5.49 each in Canada, a savings of at least 13% off the cover price. It's quite a bargain! Shipping and handling is just 50¢ per book in the U.S. and $1.25 per book in Canada.* I understand that accepting the 2 free books and gifts places me under no obligation to buy anything. I can always return a shipment and cancel at any time by calling the number below. The free books and gifts are mine to keep no matter what I decide.

Choose one: ☐ **Harlequin Desire**
(225/326 HDN GRTW)

☐ **Harlequin Presents Larger-Print**
(176/376 HDN GQ9Z)

Name (please print)

Address   Apt. #

City   State/Province   Zip/Postal Code

Email: Please check this box ☐ if you would like to receive newsletters and promotional emails from Harlequin Enterprises ULC and its affiliates. You can unsubscribe anytime.

Mail to the Harlequin Reader Service:
IN U.S.A.: P.O. Box 1341, Buffalo, NY 14240-8531
IN CANADA: P.O. Box 603, Fort Erie, Ontario L2A 5X3

Want to try 2 free books from another series? Call 1-800-873-8635 or visit www.ReaderService.com.

*Terms and prices subject to change without notice. Prices do not include sales taxes, which will be charged (if applicable) based on your state or country of residence. Canadian residents will be charged applicable taxes. Offer not valid in Quebec. This offer is limited to one order per household. Books received may not be as shown. Not valid for current subscribers to the Harlequin Presents or Harlequin Desire series. All orders subject to approval. Credit or debit balances in a customer's account(s) may be offset by any other outstanding balance owed by or to the customer. Please allow 4 to 6 weeks for delivery. Offer available while quantities last.

Your Privacy—Your information is being collected by Harlequin Enterprises ULC, operating as Harlequin Reader Service. For a complete summary of the information we collect, how we use this information and to whom it is disclosed, please visit our privacy notice located at corporate.harlequin.com/privacy-notice. From time to time we may also exchange your personal information with reputable third parties. If you wish to opt out of this sharing of your personal information, please visit readerservice.com/consumerschoice or call 1-800-873-8635. **Notice to California Residents**—Under California law, you have specific rights to control and access your data. For more information on these rights and how to exercise them, visit corporate.harlequin.com/california-privacy.

HDHP22R2

COUNTRY LEGACY COLLECTION

19 FREE BOOKS IN ALL!

Cowboys, adventure and romance await you in this new collection! Enjoy superb reading all year long with books by bestselling authors like Diana Palmer, Sasha Summers and Marie Ferrarella!